William P. Robertson (signature)

LURKING IN PENNSYLVANIA

Macabre Poetry &
Seventeen Tales of Terror
by

William P. Robertson

Copyright © 2004 by William P. Robertson

ISBN 0-7414-2150-X

Published by:

PUBLISHING.COM

1094 New Dehaven Street, Suite 100
West Conshohocken, PA 19428-2713
Info@buybooksontheweb.com
www.buybooksontheweb.com
Toll-free (877) BUY BOOK
Local Phone (610) 941-9999
Fax (610) 941-9959

Printed in the United States of America

Printed on Recycled Paper

Published August 2004

CREDITS

The stories and poems listed below were published in the following periodicals:

Stories

"Wide Spot in the Road," Dominus, Galati, Romania; "The Spirit of Catherine," Stride, Cheshire, England; "The Weight," The Glasgow Magazine, Glasgow, Scotland; "The Brown-Streaked Sidewalk," A Time for Seasons and Holidays: A Creative with Words Celebration, Carmel, CA; "When the Hunter Becomes the Hunted," Tyro Magazine, Sault Ste. Marie, Ontario, Canada; "The Golden-Rod," Prelude to Fantasy, Minneapolis, MN; "The Powers of Atahualpa," Scifant, Suisun, CA; "Fetters and Chains," The Black Abyss, Philadelphia, PA; "The Price of a Pint," Dark Starr, Oceanside, CA; "The Crimson Tinge," New Blood, Ontario, CA; "The Spirit of Catherine" and "When the Hunter Becomes the Hunted" also appeared in The Pennsylvania Reader, Wellsboro, PA. "Widespot in the Road" was also published in Vega Magazine, Bloomfield, NJ and in GW Thomas' Flashshot webzine.

Poems

"The Moor," Wicked Mystic, New York, NY; "Far Away She Waits for Me," Northern Fusion, Ingleside, Ont., Canada; "Remaining Creative," Champagne Shivers webzine; "Fear Lurked in the Shadows Here," Sepulchre, Fort Meade, MD and Haunted Hulks webzine; "Zero Hundred Hours," Shadowland, Jonesboro, GA; "Hiss N' Spit," Lunatic Chameleon, Tolland, CT; "My Mural," The Catbird Seat," Tolland, CT; "Macabre Dreams," Goddess of the Bay, Warwick, RI; "Horses," The Bradford Era, Bradford, PA.

Special thanks to David Rimer and Jill Bressan who helped edit these tales. Landscape and cover photos were taken by William P. Robertson. People photos are from the Robertson family album. Thanks also to Bonnie & Gerald Conklin for their support and encouragement. Bonnie contributed the "Fear Lurked in the Shadows Here" photograph.

MY MURAL

My mural depicts
the dark side
of the earth
where crumbling ruins
are a mecca
for blizzard shadows.
Frost beards gargoyle faces,
and sleet sheathes tombs
with black ice.
Sunshine's a controlled
substance in this clime.
Happy are the dead
who do not rise
to relive the misery
of chilblain soul
and dead legs.

AUTHOR'S NOTE

I've lived most of my life amidst the wild beauty of rural northwest Pennsylvania where hillsides choked with oak and hemlock create bleak tableaux that adversely affect one's psyche. Deserted farmhouses, overgrown graveyards, stark moors, and rusty oil field relics are just a few of the spooky features of this desolate land. In McKean, Potter, Warren, and Tioga Counties but two seasons exist--those of darkness or light. The absence of sunlight in this somber region causes some folks severe bouts of depression. For me, it inspires a dark creativity that found its outlet in the pages that follow.

I was exposed to the horror genre at an early age. My grandmother, Bernadine Johnson, came from Sweden around the turn of the 20th Century and brought with her folktales of ghosts and trolls that I found fascinating as a child. She passed down to me a love of the supernatural that my father, Paul Robertson, later nourished with his retelling of local legends. "Widespot in the Road," "The Spirit of Catherine," "The Weight," and "Antique Toys" were all inspired by stories I heard from Dad and Grandma B.

In my teenage years I was further attracted to the dark side by listening to the music of the Doors. It was also the lyrics of Jim Morrison that started my love affair with language. The "Word Man" first made me aware of the power of imagery, onomatopoeia, and alliteration before I knew the technical names for those devices. I doubt if I'd have ever written a single poem or story if not for Morrison's inspiration. I pay tribute to the Door's brand of Gothic rock in "The One and Only Price Vincent."

It was my father again who turned me on to the classic horror of Edgar Allan Poe and H.P. Lovecraft. Dad always had those authors' short story collections in his library and repeatedly urged me to delve into their work. From Poe and Lovecraft I gained a love for psychological horror and the understated scream. "When the Hunter Becomes the Hunted" and "The Goldenrod" are stories heavily influenced by the early masters.

"The Powers of Atahualpa" and "Luke the Spook" are two tales that grew out of my love of historical fiction. The first is based on Francisco Pizarro's invasion of Peru in 1531 and gives a detailed description of the Spaniard's battle plan at Cajamarca. "Luke the Spook" includes documented research of the hysteria that swept through Bradford, PA, in the fall of 1968. The phantom sighting at Willowdale Cemetery was actually observed by various persons I interviewed.

Unsettling events that plagued my own life also have served as a great inspiration. I often tried to come to terms with these traumas by weaving them into horrific tales. A good example would be "Mary and Emmett" that includes many scenes from my Uncle

Francis Larson's bout with Alzheimer's Disease. It was heartbreaking to watch Uncle France's mounting frustration as he reverted back into a child. His fits and lapses lend terrible reality to my science fantasy yarn.

Many other stories came from my everyday experiences. "The Bud Monster" was written about a neighbor's obnoxious cat that tried for years to adopt me. Likewise, "The Crimson Tinge" contains elements gleaned from my current house painting occupation. Even "Graduation Day" had humble roots, springing from a conversation I had with an old high school classmate about mid-life crisis.

While assembling this collection with the help of David Rimer and my sister, Jill Bressan, I attempted to add as much variety as possible. This led to the inclusion of "The Brown-Streaked Sidewalk"--a tale of dark humor actually experienced by my father, his brother, and his young cousin. This story is typical of the style of horror I favor. Usually, I try to chill rather than sicken. I like to stack up Gothic images to create eerie, unsettling moods. I also like endings with a twist rather than a gush of blood. Sometimes what is left unsaid is the most terrifying of all. . .

CONTENTS

THE MOOR

Out
on the moor
wasted trees
writhe
with
rigor mortis.
Catacombs
of mist
confuse & frighten
until dusk
creaks shut
with a blast
of black rain.

THE SPIRIT OF CATHERINE

Excitement had me by the throat as I slipped and skidded along the mossy rocks bordering the headwaters of Five Mile Brook. Although I had left my car well before noon, I was now just nearing my destination. I had been so immersed in fishing for scrappy little native brookies, that my exploration had taken far longer than I had anticipated. When I took apart my fly rod and hightailed it upstream, the evening shadows had already begun to creep out from beneath the hemlocks.

The scabby cherry trees seemed blacker than I had ever before seen them. The wind also began to act like the plaything of some perverse magician. Although I was an experienced woodsman, I had difficulty pinpointing from which direction it came. Its howling seemed almost cyclonic in nature and was rising fast. In the fading light only my stubbornness pushed me onward. Finally, without warning, I stumbled through an orange screen of beech leaves and skidded to a halt on the shore of the blighted swamp I had been seeking.

Having no brothers or sisters to accompany me, I had hiked alone in the woods since I was twelve. Yet, even I couldn't help but shrink from the vile sea of muck and stagnant water that stretched before me in the twilight. Great bleached tree trunks reached finger-like from the fringes of this mire, while ghostly beaver huts glowed in the mist now forming over the deeper pools. The distant chant of the whippoorwill made my face grow cold beneath my beard. If only I had asked a friend to come along. . .If only I had a friend to ask!

So this is where Catherine perished. No wonder the old Swedes wouldn't venture out here at night. According to legend, the girl had wandered off to pick Christmas ground pine and got caught in a driving blizzard. It wasn't until the following spring that her corpse was discovered by trappers near this very spot. Neighboring farmers swear that her cries for help can be heard echoing from these dark swamps even today. My grandmother said she was a winsome lass--wild as a colt and always out walking alone.

How strong the wind has grown. Yet the mist, if anything, is thicker, swirling. . .I must leave this blighted place before my imagination gets the better of me. I must turn and take one. . .step. . .at. . .a. . .time. Just one step. Oh, God! I'm sinking. . .sinking!

Catherine? Is that you? My, your skin is so cold and smooth. You are a winsome lass. Now, we shall never again have to walk through this swamp alone. . .

WIDE SPOT IN THE ROAD

Gus Carlson reined his team of horses to a halt. Staring ahead down the desolate one-lane forest track, he could feel his scalp tingle as he contemplated the hemlocks that hemmed him in like the walls of a grave. Even on the brightest summer day it was an eerie road to travel, for little sunlight ever filtered into the narrow tunnel through the trees. Today, Gus felt especially uneasy as he watched the thunderheads gather in the dark sky above and listened to the howl of the rising wind.

The horses seemed to share the farmer's uneasiness. Pulling a loaded buckboard up a five-mile grade should have tamed even the most spirited of animals. Yet, Gus suspected that the heavy lather on the black mare's flanks wasn't entirely due to physical exertion. The beast's nostrils were just too unnaturally flared as it stared off wild-eyed into the gloomy wood. Even the gentle gray rubbed uneasily against the traces and had to be prodded forward with an unusual amount of coaxing.

When the animals finally plunged ahead through the tunnel of trees, they broke into a full gallop. The buckboard jolted wildly down the slope with the farmer yanking the reins and crushing the brake for all he was worth. It wasn't until the frenzied beasts had bolted to the top of the next hillock that Gus managed to bring them under control.

Despite the biting October wind, Gus discovered that he was soaked with sweat. Perspiration poured from under his hat band and dribbled onto his spectacles. With annoyance he peeled off his glasses, mopped a coarse handkerchief across his forehead, and then proceeded to survey the distance with near-sighted eyes. From his hilltop vantage point, he could barely distinguish the blurry road ahead as it threaded its way across an infinite series of lower hillocks that rose like waves from the hemlock sea. When Gus replaced his spectacles, he noticed an ant-like vehicle moving toward him up the road three knolls away.

As Gus watched the other vehicle disappear behind the second hill, he wondered how they could ever pass on a wood-lined road barely wide enough for his own buckboard. This thought had little time to register before Gus saw the object of his concern miraculously appear atop the second knoll. This time Gus had no trouble identifying the mysterious coach. It was somber, black, and unmistakably a hearse! It was drawn by six gigantic black draft horses that trotted along as if in a trance. How the brutes were able to pull that hearse three miles in three seconds was something Gus didn't care to ponder. Instead, he urged his own

5

trembling team forward. Shortly after, to his surprise, he found a place to pull off the road and await the distant coach's arrival.

When the hearse disappeared behind the remaining hillock that separated them, Gus wondered why in ten years of traveling to market he had never before noticed this particular wide spot in the road. Nervously, he pulled at his beard and then at his watch chain. He produced an initialed timepiece that had been a gift from his eldest son, Herbert. The watch read one o'clock. It had to be later than that, Gus thought. He held the watch to his ear. It wasn't ticking. Had he forgotten to wind it that morning in his haste to get an early start? Gus twisted the winding knob and found it wouldn't move. While he replaced the broken timepiece in his pocket, a distant rumble of thunder made his horses fidget in the traces.

Gus waited for what seemed like an hour. When no vehicle appeared atop the distant knoll, the farmer muttered, "Where could that hearse have gone? There's no side roads it coulda taken. And this one's not wide enough to turn around on."

The winds rose to gale force and snatched Gus' hat from his head. As he whirled around to save it, he gasped in surprise. There, disappearing over the horizon behind him, was the somber, black coach he'd been waiting for.

Suddenly, the black mare reared up on its hind legs, and the gray emitted an almost human shriek.

6

Gus barely had time to grip the reins before his team was off and running. They never slowed until the dirt track blended into the brick highway leading into Gus' own gate.

When the buckboard swirled up the drive, Gus' wife appeared at the front door of the homestead. Her face was wan and etched with sorrow.

Visibly shaken, the farmer got down from the wagon and walked absently toward his trembling wife.

"Gus," she said blankly. "I have something to tell you."

"Yes?"

"Our son, Herbert."

"Yes?"

"H-H-He fell down the well. . .Drowned. . ."

"Around one o'clock?"

"Yes, why yes!" sobbed Gus' wife, burying her head on his shoulder. "How did you know? How could you know?"

ZERO HUNDRED HOURS

The silicon factory phantom
seeped like carbon monoxide
through the cells of the north end.
Furnaces lost loads at his passing,
and slice scrubbers screeched
like maimed mechanics.
Technicians scrambled as the
air conditioner belched frost.
Brittle laughter jumbled gauges
and froze the time clock
at zero hundred hours.

THE WEIGHT

Karl Anderson struggled with his burden. He felt his knees buckle beneath him. At this rate, he would never reach the barn that stood a good three hundred yards off through the orchard. Reeling against the nearest apple tree, he righted himself to more evenly distribute the weight on his back.

"Vhy?" he wondered aloud. "Vhy did I come out in the woods so close to dark?"

Karl was a strapping youth. At his present age of seventeen, he was already well over six-foot tall. His two hundred pounds of bulky muscle helped him perform even the most rigorous of normal farming chores. From pitching hay, to guiding a plow, to digging post holes, to shearing sheep, he was the first of his family to finish his work and the last to complain of fatigue. But then, the weight with which he now found himself saddled, could hardly be characterized as "normal."

If only he had not been so skeptical of the old legends. Those, like everything else Swedish, he believed should be cast aside now that he and his family had made a new home in America. "Vhy dvell on

9

customs from the old country?" he had asked his father countless times. "If you loved the old ways so much, vhy did you put an entire ocean betveen you and them?"

Karl had another more personal reason for spurning his heritage. He was tired of being the brunt of the American boys' jokes. Often his muscles had also come in handy when he ventured into town. At first, he had only used them when goaded into fighting by the taunt of "Dumb Swede!" That, however, was before he had thrashed every upstart farmhand within twenty miles and, in turn, had become the bully.

A faint tremor, that most would have recognized as fear, pulsed through the brawny lad as he again lurched forward toward the distant barn. He was soon forced to rest against every third tree he blundered across in the growing gloom.

Sweat poured from the immigrant boy as he leaned panting against the rough bark of a hickory trunk. Closing his eyes, he was suddenly disturbed by a very real childhood memory. It was that of his grizzled Uncle Ole sitting hunched over in his favorite rocker croaking out tales of elfin lore. Face animated with firelight, the old man had delighted in frightening the children who gathered about the hearth to hear the stories he told every Midsummer Eve. The rest of the year he was seldom known to speak more than a few mumbled words. Too shriveled to work anymore, he spent most of his hours daydreaming or limping alone through the woods to gather herbs and mushrooms. These Ole used in medicines he concocted for all the old crones of the neighborhood.

By far, his uncle's favorite stories involved the trolls--those hirsute, little men reputed to haunt the dank woodlands surrounding the Anderson farm. Karl remembered how loudly he had laughed when Ole, in the midst of his narration, would twist up his bearded cheeks in impish imitation and leap at some unsuspecting child nestled at his feet. Then the old man would describe, in hideous detail, how after sunset the Little People dropped from trees to steal a ride on a human's back. By the time Ole had explained the trolls' ultimate intent in doing so, all the children (but Karl) were crying in their mothers' aprons. These stories still would have seemed ludicrous if it had not been for the pig-like bristles scraping against the back of Karl's neck.

Karl reached the edge of the orchard just as the final glimmer of twilight was fading from the sky. Eyes blurring with fatigue, the Swede now viewed the barn as a mere shadow outlined against the horizon. With the building still a hundred yards away, he felt an overpowering urge to sink to the ground for a quick nap. Only the smell of bitterroot reminded him of the consequences.

With his endurance fading fast, Karl recognized the need for drastic action, and he became rather infuriated by the whole situation. After all, what had he to fear? Had his brawn ever failed him before in any wrestling bout? Certainly not! It had never much mattered what type of death grip his opponent used. Why should it now?

Karl reached one rope-like arm over his shoulder. Instead of throttling the unseen enemy as planned, he found his range of movement shackled by his own huge, expanding bicep. Howling in a blind animal frenzy, the immigrant whirled around and around like a bear swatting bees, clawing at the empty air. When he felt the weight grow tighter to him still, he wildly butted his back against the next gnarled tree he encountered in the dusk. Each time he rebounded into the air, an electric shock wave exploded in his brain.

Finally, everything went blank, and Karl slumped to his knees. The next thing he knew, he was instinctively stumbling in a dead run toward the barn. The brief contact with the ground had proven true his Uncle Ole's elfin lore. No blackout could compare with the empty nothingness felt when one's soul is being slowly sucked away.

Karl was now totally consumed by fear. Nor had he ever before felt so alone. It was as if he were rushing headlong down a subterranean tunnel to hell. He could no longer feel his legs, but he knew they must be working when the deeper shadows surrounding the barn loomed up to engulf him.

With the radar of a bat, Karl veered off at a right angle to the barn wall and followed it along until he distinguished the faint glow of lantern light leaking from the bottom of a side door. He lifted the latch and ducked his giant frame through the four-and-a-half foot opening that had been purposely built that size by his superstitious father. As he did so, he heard a thump behind him and whirled in time to see an impish figure leap up and flee into the night. All at once, the weight was gone from Karl's back. If only it had left his heart, as well. The imp had had his Uncle Ole's face.

THE BROWN-STREAKED SIDEWALK

As the three boys squeezed through the crowd and out of the circus tent, their air of gaiety vanished. They had just spent three joy-filled hours giggling at clowns, oo-oo-ing at trapeze performers, and clapping (between big bites of cotton candy) at the elephant acts. Now, the time had come for the long trek home across town in the dark.

Buster, the eldest, assumed command once they left behind the smoky brilliance of the Big Top. He was a hulking youth of thirteen, and a sadistic grin gleamed briefly on his rough features as he glanced back at his younger brother, Lenny. The little squirt had his ball cap crammed down over his forehead, concealing all but his very round eyes. Dogging the heels of Buster's pal, Pete, he concentrated fully upon tracing the older boys' footsteps in the growing gloom.

Being a tag-along was about all that Lenny was good for. It seemed to Buster that he couldn't go anywhere without the little goof. And what made matters worse, their mother now expected him to drag Lenny along at night too. Cripe, how were he and Pete going to meet girls if they had to wet-nurse the Squirt all the time? Well, maybe if everything went okay on the way home. . .

To reach the distant lighted street, the boys had to cross a parking lot bordered by an abandoned baseball stadium. This ballpark once housed the Pony League team noted for developing such pitching stars as Elroy Face and Warren Spahn. But there hadn't been a night game there for years, and now its peeling green walls and ramshackle clubhouse created a pool of midnight that even quickened patrolling policemen on their appointed rounds. Needless to say, the boys avoided these deeper shadows as long as possible while circling the outer perimeter of the stadium.

Finally, they arrived at a murky tunnel that ran between the left field wall and a boundary fence. Here, Buster winked at Pete before deliberately quickening the pace. As planned, the moment they were totally immersed in darkness, they were off and sprinting for the safety of the streetlights, two hundred yards in the distance.

It took Lenny awhile to realize he was alone in the dark. He fumbled blindly along, groping for Pete's shirt sleeves and whimpering softly to himself. Ten steps into the blackness, he finally dared peek out from under the brim of his ball cap.

A squeal pierced the night like a hatchet blade. Pete and Buster nodded meaningfully to one another and then glanced up from where they stood panting against a lamppost. It wasn't long before they

15

perceived a dim shape streaking around the corner of the stadium toward them.

Lenny emerged from the shadows hatless and out of breath. His face was pasty. His eyes glittered with fear. He gave no sign of recognition as he wheeled toward the older boys. If they hadn't grabbed him, he would have barreled into the path of an oncoming Studebaker.

"What ails you?" howled Buster as he struggled to restrain his brother. "Where's your hat?"

Lenny stared wildly at his captors and then nodded toward the eerie, dark tunnel.

"Hey, Squirt, you're not gonna leave it there, I hope. When we get home, you'll get a lickin' if you do!"

"I d-d-d-don't care!"

"Say, what?" bullied Buster. "Why, I. . .I think you're chicken!"

The squirt flinched at the most dreaded word in a small fry's vocabulary, but he did not deny the accusation. Instead, he anchored himself to the lamppost in anticipation of his antagonists' next move.

"Don't tell us you're afraid of the dark," smirked Pete. "Are you afraid the boogeyman will get you?"

"Yeah, if you think you're big enough to hang out with us, you'd better get your butt back in there and get that hat!"

Except to tighten his grip on the lamppost, Lenny still did not move. Only after contemplating the murder in Buster's eye, did he squeak, "Okay. . .but you gotta go with me."

The older boys glanced warily into the pit of blackness bordering the stadium before echoing, "G-G-Go with you?"

"S-S-Sure. . ."

"You gotta be kiddin'," muttered Pete.

"Ah. . .heck!" growled Buster, staring red-faced at his watch. "It's gettin' late. . .Forget the cap. Let's just get outta here."

When Lenny, Pete, and Buster dashed from the stadium parking lot, it was already well past eleven o'clock. Now, instead of taking the long, safe way home, they were forced to cut through the town oil refinery to make up for lost time. Straying from the well-lighted boulevard, they stumbled along a set of greasy railroad tracks between oil tanks two stories high. As they moved farther into the complex, refinery towers loomed up large, hissing steam and casting flickery flames across their path. With each new flare-up, Lenny dug his claws into the back of his brother's jacket and shut his eyes until they hurt. He was too scared to notice Pete's similar reaction.

Finally, even Buster could take it no longer. Catching a glimpse of the streetlights at the far end of the refinery yard, he shook his brother loose and broke into a gallop, with Pete close behind. By the time the bawling Lenny had caught up with them, Buster was as self-composed as ever and standing on East Main Street. "What took you so long, Squirt?" he sneered.

17

Lenny dug his dirty knuckles into his eyes, precipitating a fresh flood of tears. "Why did you guys leave me back there?" he blubbered.

"Ah, shut up, you baby!" snarled Pete.

"Yeah," said Buster. "What are you gonna do when we get to the witch house if you're scared now?"

"W-W-W-Witch house?"

"You know. The one up at the end of the block. Gee, I thought all big boys heard of that place."

The house to which Buster referred had terrorized town kids for over twenty years. It sat isolated on a bank overlooking East Main Street and was in a sorry state of disrepair. The porch was rotten, the shutters hung at crazy angles, and only the attic window was intact. It was there that "many a witch sighting" had been made, according to Pete.

"Yeah," added Buster, wishing to enlighten his brother. "Let me tell you all about it."

And tell him about it, he did. For the next twenty minutes, as they scurried along the gloomy tree-lined street, the bully conjured up tales of evil-eyed hags and disappearing neighbor boys that left Lenny a quivering mess of twitching nerve ends. When at last they reached the opening in the trees occupied by the witch house, Buster was just finishing his most ghastly tale of all. With a wicked smile, he pointed up the hill and said, by way of conclusion, "And up there, in that very window, they could see the old witch hacking up Jimmy Jones' body with a butcher knife this long!"

Buster made an exaggerated gesture and then glanced in the direction he had just pointed. When his eyes focused on a green face leering at him from the attic, he heard Pete gurgle a warning before sprinting off down the street. The hairs on Buster's neck bristled, and he leaped straight in the air. The next instant, he was streaking off in the same direction taken by his pal.

Half-way down the block Pete again came into sight, and Buster began to gain steadily on him. Just as he was about to overtake him, he felt a rush of wind and looked up to see the little squirt, Lenny, zoom past and disappear up the next hill.

Blinking with astonishment, Buster muttered, "What the. . .How the. . ."

It was then that he noticed the brown streak up the sidewalk.

MENACING SHADOW MEN

Transports trundle from the dusk.
Death squads erupt into the oak,
probing with red laser beams
and high tech scouts.
The wind retreats through the trees,
gasping like a lung-shot beast.
Bark eyelids snap shut
as menacing shadow men
root for the spirit of the forest.

WHEN THE HUNTER BECOMES THE HUNTED

The ridge grew appreciably steeper. Frank took two more weary steps and then plopped exhausted onto a fallen log. Despite his fatigue, there was a determined glimmer in his eyes, and his right hand never strayed far from the high-powered rifle cradled in the crook of his arm. Even clad in bulky wool hunting garb, the gaunt man looked like a stick figure against the background of snow.

The hunter glanced at his feet and contemplated his heavy, insulated boots. No wonder I'm beat, he thought. I must be wearing at least twenty pounds of clothing. God, how does Boss keep up such a pace? Who does he think he is, anyway? Daniel stinking Boone?

The man Frank had been tracking through the snow was chief architect at Wright's Construction and Frank's hated superior. His real name was Dwight M. Stone III, but everyone--including the owner of the company--called him Boss. He had earned his nickname mainly through his gruff manner and the dread he instilled in his crew with his cold, amber eyes. Jimmy, the office clerk, best characterized their effect when he exclaimed after a nasty reprimand, "Sometimes Boss makes me feel like a roast cooking on a spit!"

What made Boss' hold over others complete was a powerful build that dwarfed that of even the most muscle-bound bricklayer on the payroll. Yet, the puzzling part was how he kept in such good condition. He didn't swim. He didn't pump iron at the Y. He didn't even play on the company's flag football team. And for someone who had no time for jogging, it was amazing how he had been able to stride up over this hogback without pausing once for a breather.

As Frank puzzled over these mysteries, he glanced down the gully he had just scaled at the tangle of moss-covered rocks and fallen logs that had sent him sprawling numerous times during his ascent. Unfortunately, the terrain ahead looked even more broken. The thickly wooded ridge rose steadily before leveling off into a hemlock and laurel-choked hilltop. Stumbling to his feet, the hunter soon discovered that Boss' track, like that of some pursued beast, led off into the densest part of this thicket.

Frank lowered his head and bulled along thinking how foolish he had been to follow Boss. Jealousy, that's all it was! Jealousy and a desire to know what made him the most successful hunter at camp every year. So what if the SOB did choose to hunt alone? Was it a crime that he refused to take part in their drives or to even stand on point while the deer were driven past him?

Yet, how nervous Boss always got the night before the hunt. The way he prowled about the camp keeping everyone awake, one would have thought he was the quarry. And that beard-growing ritual of his was equally ridiculous. While most guys didn't shave the weekend before buck season, Boss started his growth a whole month ahead of everyone else, saying it brought him luck. By the time the first day rolled around, his face was a mass of matted fur that concealed every feature but those damned amber eyes. If anything, they grew even more piercing as the day of the hunt drew near.

Frank paused to examine Boss' dim boot tracks. In the heart of the thicket, they had become increasingly difficult to follow. Besides the sheer density of the laurel, matters were complicated by the patches of bare granite protruding from the snow. In places Boss was able to go over fifty yards at a time without leaving a single track. When that happened, Frank was forced to circle until he again picked up the trail. Two-thirds the way through the tangle of brush, Frank lost it altogether. It was here that he found Boss' cap, coat, and rifle cached beneath a fallen hemlock.

"Damn!" muttered Frank as he examined the other hunter's gear. "What does Boss do, run down a buck and stab it to death with his knife?"

Head bobbing like an agitated turkey, Frank glanced nervously into the thicket before chuckling grimly to himself. "Why, he can't do that! That's illegal! Maybe once I'm clear of this pucker brush, I'll catch the stinking outlaw and turn him in. What will old man Wright think of his precious Boss then?"

Frank bolted through the remaining tangle of laurel, emerging totally exhausted. Toppling forward into the snow, he didn't even attempt to protect his rifle. When his dizziness passed, he opened his eyes and unsuccessfully scanned the ridge below him for Boss. It wasn't for several minutes that he noticed the huge set of canine tracks into which he had collapsed.

Frank scrambled to his haunches and examined the prints more closely. "What the hell?" he wondered aloud. "These are either the biggest dog tracks I've ever seen, or a wolf's! But there haven't been any wolves around here in over a hundred years. And those were Lobos, not the big timber variety. Man, these look just like the ones I saw outside my sanitarium window."

As Frank got to his feet to poke the snow from the barrel of his rifle, he felt very cold despite his recent exertion. Picking up the fresh trail, he slunk along, eyes aglitter, scanning every patch of brush capable of hiding a red squirrel. Whenever he paused to catch his breath, he kept his back against a tree and his rifle ready to fire. I'll bet this is exactly the way Boss would proceed, he thought.

The beast made no attempt whatsoever to hide its track. Frank followed it with ease over the ridge and into a little hollow that was usually teeming with deer. Proof of that he found in the form of a badly mauled doe lying dead across the trail. Its throat was severed and slash marks bloodied its flank. Half-eaten entrails hung from a hole gnawed in its side. By the small amount of deer hair scattered about the snow, Frank knew it couldn't have put up much of a struggle. Whatever had killed it, be it dog or wolf, had overpowered the poor beast with a strength that Frank cared not to witness firsthand.

With a shiver, the hunter slipped his rifle off safe and backtracked until he had located the point of ambush. Frank soon discovered the imprint of the canine's body where it had laid upwind and above the well-traveled deer trail. He even saw where it had propelled itself onto the back of its prey. The funny part was, that's where its trail ended! There were plenty of hoof marks left by the staggering doe, but the big dog prints had absolutely vanished.

Frank fearfully scanned the hemlock branches around him and then backed slowly out of the hollow, his knuckles white on his gunstock. As he retreated up the ridge, his thoughts suddenly returned to Boss. What if he should encounter this beast? Frank gloated. What chance would even Boss have? That'd fix the SOB for recommend-ing me for psychological testing. I'd welcome the sight of him mutilated along the trail!

Cackling to himself, Frank strode toward the thicket where several hours ago he had lost Boss' track. Although this route was tougher going, it would shorten his journey back to camp by at least an hour. With any luck, he might even get out of the woods before twilight faded from the gloomy December sky.

The hunter plunged frantically through the undergrowth, dogged by the lengthening shadows. The faster he hurried, the more he tripped over the gnarled laurel roots and slipped on broken granite. Soon he was bruised, limping, and drenched with sweat. When he had about reached the limit of his endurance, his senses were jarred by a series of hoarse grunts echoing from the laurel ahead.

Frank collapsed into the kneeling position and wrapped his sling around his left arm. Even that didn't steady his rifle as he sighted down the barrel in anticipation of the mad snarling rush of the cur that now stalked him. He planned to fire only at the last possible instant to insure the bullet's optimum shocking power. He dare not miss. In these close quarters he may only hold together long enough for one shot.

The brush rattled, and the hunter's finger tightened on the trigger. Just one more step. . .One more. . .

There was a grunt. The brush parted, and Frank's trigger finger froze in mid-squeeze. Instead of a blood-crazed beast, out stepped Boss hauling behind him his latest fresh-killed trophy buck. Fixing the other with his cold, amber eyes, he said, "Getting a little jumpy, aren't you, Frank? I didn't think they let you carry a gun anymore."

26

Flushing, Frank lowered his rifle and got stiffly to his feet. He always felt five years old whenever Boss chided him. That was what made working for him such a strain. Especially annoying to Frank was Boss' habit of hovering over his drawing board whenever he worked with ink. How was anyone supposed to produce his best work with old Vulture Eyes practically perched on his shoulder?

"Nice b-b-b-buck," Frank finally stammered. "Where did you g-g-get him?"

"Over there," snapped Boss, jerking a thumb behind him. He was now fully clothed and had his own weapon slung over his shoulder.

"In the middle of all that laurel? Say. . .was that your stuff I found cached back there?"

"Yep. I found a cave I wanted to explore. The only way I could squeeze inside was to leave behind my coat and gun."

"What time did you shoot your buck?"

"Oh, I got him about half-hour ago."

"Funny. I didn't hear you f-f-fire."

"The wind must have been blowing in the wrong direction."

"M-M-Maybe you're right. Let me get a closer look at those horns."

As Frank lurched forward, Boss stepped squarely in his path. "Oh, no," he growled. "You're not walking behind me with a loaded rifle. You'll have plenty of time to admire the buck's head when I get it mounted.

It'll be hanging in the office soon enough with all the others. I'm surprised they let you come back to work after you pinned my hand to your drawing board with that damn compass. I wouldn't have sent you to Canada for a little <u>vacation</u>. I'd have put you away for good!"

"H-H-How do you know where the company sent me to. . .rest?" asked Frank while thoughts of those huge canine tracks outside the sanitarium flashed through his mind.

"Don't worry. I have my ways. Now back off!"

With a whimper Frank stumbled backward after catching a quick glimpse of the dead deer. It had the same gnawed throat as the doe he had found down the trail.

"Boss, this may sound crazy, b-b-but did you see a. . .wolf. . .out here today?"

A smile spread over Boss' lupine face, and a flash of white teeth showed in his beard. "I think you better get back to camp now," he said in a condescending whisper. "I don't need your help dragging out my kill. It will be dark soon. Yes. Very, very soon. . ."

THE CRIMSON TINGE

Johnny pulled up in front of a purple mansion that sat sandwiched between two vacant brick homes. The painter did not shut off the motor right away but sat surveying the three-story dwelling with a professional eye and a foot poised over the gas pedal. He had heard all the wild rumors about the place, and he had a hard time disbelieving their validity as he studied the garish purple walls and barred windows. It didn't help matters that the rising sun shone directly on the freshly painted house front, accenting its odd crimson tinge.

Johnny ran his hand across the two-day stubble sprouting on his face before turning off the ignition. A rumpled ball cap covered his unruly shock of snowy hair, and his soiled painter's clothes were dotted with faded splotches of tan and blue. "Shouldn'ta took this gold-durn job," he grumbled as he climbed down from the patched seat of his pickup and hobbled around to yank open the sagging tailgate.

The truth of the matter was that Johnny hadn't worked all summer and was in no position to turn it down. He had botched several jobs the painters' union had set up for him earlier in the year, and they had pretty much written him off. . .until now. They had also conveniently failed to tell him that everyone else at the union hall had passed on this particular assignment after the first two painters had mysteriously disappeared from town. All that Johnny knew was that he had received $1,000 in advance just to finish part of a back wall!

Johnny hoisted a forty-foot ladder from the rack atop his pickup and weaved beneath its weight toward the spiked fence that surrounded the house. Fortunately, the gate had been left open, and he moved cautiously through it and then past six heavily curtained, barred windows around to the back of the house. The lawn felt spongy as cemetery grass beneath his feet.

With a grunt, the old man dropped the ladder and raised his eyes to study the back wall of the house. The other painters had scraped the entire surface with an expert skill far beyond that now capable of his stringy muscles and creaking joints. They had even burned off some of the more stubborn chipped spots before priming and painting the back peak. Their work had stopped just above a curious, oval, stained glass window located two-thirds the way up the clapboard wall. Amber in hue, it was approximately three feet wide and five feet high. It was also the only window on that side of the house and the only one with no bars or curtains.

It took all the old man's strength to hoist the

ladder into position well away from the window. "Get the gold-durn thing eventually," he muttered while returning to his truck to retrieve a four-inch brush, two gallons of paint, and a drop cloth to spread on the ground beneath the ladder. Sure it was against standard procedure to do the lower part of the wall before finishing the window, but Johnny figured he might as well get the grunt work out of the way first.

Johnny knelt at the foot of the ladder and opened one of the unlabeled paint cans with his putty knife. Then he withdrew a wooden stick from his coveralls and mixed the paint with an unhurried lifting motion. It took many minutes of patient stirring to blend in the queer, crimson swirl that had separated from the rest of the mixture and accounted for its abnormal hue. If this paint had not been sent with his $1,000 check, Johnny knew he wouldn't have been able to match it with any enamel he'd run across in 40 years.

"Musta had the gold-durn stuff imported," reasoned the old man as he examined the contents of the unlabeled can once more before starting up the ladder behind him. When he reached the top, he fished in his coveralls and produced an s-shaped hook that he employed to hang his paint pail from a convenient ladder rung. Then he pulled a brush from another pocket and began applying the paint in long, smooth, practiced strokes. One coat covered the clapboards within his reach, and he climbed down to move the ladder closer to the window. He repeated the procedure twice more until he was two feet from the amber orb. At that point, he swung the ladder two feet to the other side of the window and continued across the side of the house. Afterward, he moved the ladder below the window to the next tier down. By so avoiding the fine trim work, he was able to finish the entire back wall by lunchtime.

Johnny returned to his pickup and snapped open a dented lunch pail. Since his wife died in '82, he had lived primarily on junk food, and today was no exception. As he wolfed down a bag of potato chips and a cold can of greasy spaghetti, he sat contemplating the crimson-tinged purple house with an unexplainable dread. There was just something about that color that gave even an unimaginative man like Johnny the heebie-jeebies.

Shifting his gaze from the gaudy porch to the barred windows above it, the painter could have sworn that he saw the curtains part and then quickly reclose. With a shiver, he tossed the half-eaten can of spaghetti back into his lunch pail and rooted under the seat for a trim brush. He produced a paint-caked screwdriver, three pop bottles, and a moldy submarine sandwich before he finally located one.

"Time to get this gold-durn place done and get the hell outta here," growled Johnny when he returned to his work station and stared up at the two-foot unpainted strip of clapboard surrounding the single window. "Gonna be a bitch, but I gotta do her!"

Johnny adjusted the ladder and raised it even with the top of the window. After restirring the paint, he climbed upward until he could reach the unpainted circle to the right of the amber orb. Then he dipped his brush, wiped away the excess purple globs, and proceeded to, as they say in the painters' trade, "cut in" the stained glass pane. Although his hand shook with palsy, he used a skill gained through forty years of experience to deftly complete the task.

The old painter moved the ladder to the left of the window but did not scale it right away. Instead, he walked around the yard on his toes to stretch his aching arches and calf muscles. What he really needed was a quick nap, but somehow the thought of sleeping in the lengthening shadows of that odd-colored house wasn't exactly appealing. Also, the sky had become more overcast as the afternoon progressed, and the sun disappeared behind the clouds with alarming frequency. It was this observation that finally prodded Johnny back to work. One thing was for sure. He definitely didn't want to get rained off and have to return tomorrow!

While Johnny began to reclimb the ladder, the sun emerged from the clouds and reflected blindingly from the clapboards back into his eyes. Dazedly, he squinted toward the amber window to get his bearings. It was at that exact moment that the sun again dipped out of sight.

Johnny found himself staring straight into the center of the stained glass pane which, upon closer observation, was constructed in imitation of a human eye. Looking in through the pupil, he could distinctly see an attic loft of considerable dimension. Hanging upside down from the rafters of the vaulted ceiling were two human forms dressed in painters' coveralls. Tubes ran from each of the dangling arms into open paint cans on the floor.

Johnny grew faint and slumped forward against the ladder. As he did so, he dropped his bucket, spilling its contents down the side of the house. Clutching madly at the rungs above him, he managed to right himself. Before he fully regained his senses, he felt an added weight on the ladder below him. Somehow, he dared not look down. . .

REMAINING CREATIVE

Remaining creative requires strong fear
The whisper of witches inside of your ear
Full moon neurosis controlling the brain
Lunatic lovers who drive you insane
The dripping of faucets that cannot be fixed
The drinking of potions that shouldn't be
mixed
Remaining creative's a bane and a curse
Visions, revisions, a ride in a hearse

THE ONE AND ONLY PRICE VINCENT

The young guitarist bent scowling over his instrument. He had stayed up all night to compose a song, and it was easy to tell by the sullenness of his eyes that he was far from satisfied with the results. As he strummed the catchy chords over and over, his mind fumbled vaguely for suitable lyrics.

Just as the guitarist was about to give up in frustration, the front door swung open and in strode a hip, bearded young man with several sheets of typing paper clutched tightly in his hand. With him from the street, he brought the echoes of a waking city pulsing into life.

"What's shakin', dude?" asked the visitor. "Hey, that sounds like a really happenin' tune you're workin' on."

"Yeah, Willard," grunted the guitarist with a thin smile. "It's gonna be a million-seller. I just know it."

"You've hit on a good riff, all right. Say, if you haven't got any lyrics yet, why don't you take a look at these, Price? I like wrote all five of them last night before I crashed out. Talk about a creative burst!"

Willard perched on a stool next to Price Vincent

and handed him the neatly typed lyric sheets he had gotten up early to prepare. With surprise he noted the hard look that passed over the latter's face when he snatched them up.

"Hey, Price, just from the portion of your song I overheard, I'm sure the words to my 'Hannah' will fit it perfectly. Check it out, dude!"

The guitarist leafed through the pages until he found the one Willard was so enthused about. Halfheartedly, he skimmed through it before tossing the whole pile of lyrics to the floor beside him. Without a word, he sprang from his stool and slammed his instrument in its case. He was careful Willard did not see the jealous hatred burning in his eyes when he bolted for the control room.

After his partner had stamped away in silence, Willard rescued one of the typed sheets from the floor and followed after him. "Hey, you didn't tell me what you thought of 'H-H-Hannah,'" he stammered, laying his lyric on the control board where Price would be sure to see it. "If you don't like that one, I'll be glad to help you revise anything you've already started."

"Don't be so damn pushy!" snapped Vincent. "I'm nearly finished, and I don't need your help!"

"Hey, what's wrong with you lately, man? It seems like every time I make a suggestion, you take my head off."

"Don't you think I'm capable of writing my own lyrics? Didn't I compose the band's first big hit, 'Rivers of Blood?'"

Willard leaned against a filing cabinet and stared hard at his friend, who hovered over the control board with his back toward him. Price's shoulder-length hair concealed the sides of his face, shielding the dark thoughts that lurked there.

"Hey, why won't you work with me anymore?" squeaked the lyricist. "I wrote over fifty lyrics in the past six months, and you've used only one of them." To emphasize his point, Willard jerked open the bottom drawer of the filing cabinet and revealed a veritable treasure trove of his material. "Why do you think I penned all these? For the sake of mental exercise? Look at me, man!"

Price mumbled something under his breath but did not turn around.

"Man, you know I write topnotch stuff! After all, haven't I won prizes for my work in international competitions? Haven't I?"

The guitarist stiffened at his partner's crowing. Willard had been bragging about those prizes for months. In an effort to keep his cool, Vincent snatched up a screwdriver and began drumming it against the face of the control board. *If only Willard will shut up,* he thought. *I'm much too tired to deal with this hassle now. I need sleep, bad. I--*

"Price, I need to know now! When do you plan to start using my material again? Don't forget that I've been doing all the grunt work for you and the

Electrocutioners for like eight years. Yeah, from the beginning I've been your lyricist, roadie, and publicity agent. Now that we're on the verge of national stardom, it seems like a rather poor time to cut me off. Sure your one song was our first hit single, but you don't have to be greedy. How do you expect me to benefit financially if you don't release any of my material? After all the hard work I put into this band, I deserve better!"

The guitarist still did not answer. Instead, he surveyed the outer studio through the plexiglass window above the control board. As he took note of the stack of amplifiers piled up next to the front door in readiness for that night's gig, he thought about how much sweat and money he himself had funneled into the band. Had he not taken out personal loans for the equipment truck, PA system, and studio recording deck? Had he not--

"Hey, Price, hey! Answer me!" shouted Willard into his partner's ear. He was now so furious that his voice rose to a piercing, obnoxious pitch. There was also a nasty gleam in his eyes as he continued: "Price, if you're not reasonable about this, I'm left with no alternative. You know how the copyright forms are set up to include each author and his contribution? Well, if you remember, we weren't required to tell which individual songs were co-written and which were not. That means that as far as the boys in Washington are concerned, I helped you with every single tune on our last copyright tape. Yeah, I'm gonna swear I'm the co-author even if you did write all but one song yourself. Dig?"

Price's eyes widened in acknowledgment. "Like hell!" he roared, spinning around to bury the screwdriver he had been fingering into his partner's throat.

A gurgle of surprise splashed from Willard's crushed voice box. Then he toppled over backward, blood spurting from the hole in his larynx. With his last gasp of breath, he watched horrified as Price grabbed his lyric "Hannah" from the control board and torched it with a lighter.

A vicious leer burned on Vincent's face while he watched the paper burn down to his fingertips. He dropped the charred embers to the floor and stamped them out furiously with his left foot. Afterward, he glanced madly about the studio chanting, "What to do with the body? The body. The body. What to do with the body? Now, that I freed its dark soul! Why, that's it. The lyrics. The lyrics I searched for all night! Yeah, what can I do with you, Willard? Now, that I freed your black soul?"

It was just minutes before showtime, and electricity was in the air. While Price adjusted his guitar strap, he glanced across the darkened stage toward the shadowy figures of roadies who scurried back and forth adjusting sound monitors and setting up mike stands. Red amplifier eyes and lit cigarettes glowed in the murk. Although Price couldn't distinguish his drummer, he knew that he had assumed his position behind his kit by the muffled tattoo of drum sticks rattling from snare to tom to cymbal and back again. As the drummer went through his paces, the guitarist quivered with the excitement felt by boxers before a championship bout. After all, wasn't performing life's ultimate high!!

When two shadows glided toward their microphones to Price's right, he strode over to his amplifier and plugged in his guitar. At that moment the audience flickered with the gleam of a thousand Zippo lighters held head-high by the impatient crowd. He was about to join his bassist centerstage when the head roadie grabbed him by the arm and whispered, "Hey, Price, have you seen Willard? He was supposed to show up tonight and run the follow spot."

"Yeah, he's around here somewhere, but I don't think he'll be of much help."

"Why not?"

"He's been having some trouble with his throat."

"What does that have to do with him helping with the light show?" grumbled the roadie.

"Hey, that's not my problem! Do the best you can!" snarled Vincent as he shook himself free from the other's grasp. "Willard may show up later, but I doubt it."

Before the roadie could protest further, there

was a blinding burst of light. Flashpots exploding near the front of the stage bathed the band in eerie crimson. The kids in the audience squealed with unbridled delight when the M.C. shouted above the din, "Ladies and gentlemen, it is with great pleasure that on behalf of the Fairfield College student government, I present the one and only Price Vincent and the Electrocutioners!"

Right on cue, Price leaped forward into the spotlight that appeared centerstage. Cranking his guitar to five, he laid down some nasty licks. With the rest of band blasting away behind him, he danced and gyrated like a madman undergoing electroshock therapy. He did a split at the exact moment the stage again exploded with flashpot fire.

The louder the audience howled its approval, the louder Vincent cranked his guitar. By midway through the set, he had the dial turned to eight as he boogied his way through a Rolling Stones' oldie, "Satisfaction." He and his bassist began bumping to the beat and pumping their instruments in a suggestive fashion. When the rhythm section settled into a pulsing groove, Price screamed into the microphone, "Have any of you people ever loved someone who wouldn't even fart in your face? Well, I have!"

"Me, too," chirped the bassist, "and it ain't no fun!"

"Well, what can a dude do about it?" growled Price. "You don't know? Well, let me tell ya! When your baby don't wantcha, you gotta do what ya gotta do. Know what that it?"

"N-o-o-o!!" echoed the crowd.

"You gotta get out the Jack. The Jack Daniels. When you and he become real familiar, you gotta, you gotta walk right up to your baby. That's right! You gotta walk right up to her and say, 'BA-BYYY, I WANNA JUMP YER BONES!"

There was absolute bedlam as 10,000 howling fans expressed their personal satisfaction. To compensate for the noise level, Price again adjusted the volume control on his guitar. Cranking it up to ten, he danced into the spotlight that appeared once more centerstage. He struck five impressive chords by windmilling his right arm and then raised both fists over his head in a gesture of triumph. At that exact instant a shower of sparks erupted from Vincent's guitar, and he jerked convulsively forward, toppling over his mike stand. As he wobbled to his knees, the audience was on its feet for a rousing ovation. It wasn't until the drummer had pounced from behind his kit to unplug Price's amp, that the crowd began to realize the guitarist's condition wasn't part of the act.

Suddenly, the curtain tumbled down, and the stage was awash with roadies and security guards who gathered around Price as he writhed and contorted, near death. The head roadie even had the presence of mind to check the guitarist's amplifier. When he noticed that the back was loose, he produced a screwdriver from his pocket and removed the cover. He was greeted by a horrible stench. Gagging, he backed away in search of reinforcements. He returned with a security guard in tow, and they spun the amp farther away from the stage wall to have a look inside. Their flashlight beams revealed the charred remains of a severed human hand lodged against a shorted transformer tube.

With the stench of burnt flesh strong in his nostrils, the head roadie remembered his conversation with Price before the show. On a hunch, he stumbled over to the towering bass cabinet and pried off the cover. The security guard had gone to vomit. Maybe it was just as well he didn't stick around, for the roadie was about to discover how a simple case of throat trouble had kept Willard from his light crew duties. What no one would be able to explain was the vengeful smile that gleamed so horribly from the lyricist's decapitated head.

THE POWER OF ATAHUALPA

Francisco Pizarro crouched in the shadowy doorway and stared out at the sunbleached stone houses that surrounded the great square of Cajamarca. Through the city gates he could discern the Inca legions approaching across the plain. Pizarro pulled nervously at his pointed beard as he watched the horde swell, the sun glinting from the golden ornaments of the noblemen, the Orejones. The dark Andes Mountains rose ominously in the far distance, blocking any hope of retreat. These snow-capped peaks made the prospects of the impending battle seem even grimmer to the worried Spaniard.

Pizarro's stern, lined face relaxed only a little as he reviewed his battle plan once more in his head. Against sixty to one odds, he knew that the conquistadors' only chance of survival lie in capturing the Inca king, Atahualpa. To achieve that end, he had deployed his men in places of ambush throughout Cajamarca. His two cavalry commanders, Hernando De Soto and Hernando Pizzaro, had been positioned inside two great stone halls facing the square. The doorways of these buildings were easily spacious enough for a mounted rider to pass through. In another hall he had placed his twenty crossbow men along with those few armed with muskets. As for himself, after overseeing the deployment of two small cannons on a tower overlooking the square, he had chosen a party of twenty of the company's best swordsmen to lead into battle.

A clash of armor in the dimly lighted hall roused Francisco Pizzaro from his reverie. He stared once more at the approaching menace. The advancing army had now drawn within two hundred yards of the city gates, and the conquistador licked his dry lips greedily as the golden litter that bore Atahualpa passed within view. Preceding the king came a corps of servants who swept all rubbish from his path with long-handled brooms. Another company of high-ranking nobles crowded closely about the royal litter to form a human shield between the Spanish enemy and Atahualpa. These men were easily distinguished by the huge plugs of gold that adorned their ear lobes.

Pizarro smiled grimly to himself as he wondered why that heathen wretch, Atahualpa, was held in such awe by his people. He had heard all the legends through the interpreter but failed to comprehend how even ignorant Indians could believe that their king was actually descended from the sun. He also scoffed at the reports of the Inca's great power to instill fear in the bosoms of men. No one would ever catch him, Francisco Pizarro, crawling to an audience with any heathen. He would not be afraid to look Atahualpa square in the eye when the time came. Let savages quiver at the thought of looking into the eye of the sun!

Pizarro's thoughts did not shift from Atahualpa until the column of Inca warriors began to file through the city gates and line up along the sides of the square. They were now close enough for Pizarro to note their quilted cotton body armor and the geometric designs painted on their square hide shields. He was also surprised to see them so lightly armed with star-headed maces or double-edged wooden swords. Not one soldier of the six thousand that entered Cajamarca carried a sling or a spear. Chanting victory songs, they apparently believed they had little to fear from the Spanish who, as reported by their scouts, "cowered" inside the halls around them.

Suddenly, the singing ceased. The golden litter of Atahualpa appeared in the square, bore upon the shoulders of eight brawny bearers. As it approached, Pizarro was absolutely dazzled by the Inca's display of wealth. Sunlight sparkled from two high arches of gold set with precious stones that formed the framework for a cloth canopy over the litter. Inside, the Inca sat upon a golden throne that befitted a god. He was attired in a richly woven tunic, and the royal fringe, or borla, adorned his dark hair. Pizarro couldn't distinguish a single feature of his adversary's face because of the golden light that flashed from an enormous medallion dangling from the Inca's neck.

When the litter came to a halt, a complete,

47

reverent hush fell over the square until Atahualpa's voice rang out, harsh and demanding. This was the signal Pizarro had awaited, and he immediately nodded to two figures that crouched behind him in the darkness of the hall. A dusty friar and an Indian interpreter reluctantly stumbled to their feet and shuffled out the doorway. Pizarro watched them proceed to the foot of the Inca's litter where they stood hesitantly blinking up at the heathen. The friar's mission was to convert Atahualpa to the true faith, Christianity. If the Inca would only see the light, bloodshed could yet be averted.

Pizarro wasn't close enough to understand the meek words of the interpreter, but he could tell by the furious tone of the Inca king's response that all was not going well. Finally, Pizarro saw the friar cross himself and hand his Bible up to Atahualpa. The heathen turned it one way then the other, leafed furiously through its pages, and flung it into the dust. The friar stood mortified for a second, scooped the holy book to his breast, and then scurried for the shelter of the nearest building. At that moment Pizarro emerged from his place of hiding and waved a white scarf.

There was a single signal shot. Then the square erupted with thunder and flames as the tower cannons rained grapeshot down upon the Incas. Warriors were struck down as if by magic, and a panic--that was greatly heightened by the scattered fire of the rifle and crossbow--surged through the ranks.

Just as the Indians began to recover from the reeling cannon blasts, the cavalry galloped from the halls that concealed them and burst into the melee shouting, "Santiago and at them!" All who stood in the horsemen's path were either cut down or trampled, and the clanging of the steeds' breastplates and neck bells so terrified the Incas that they abandoned their weapons altogether. Soon piles of dead littered every corner of the square and blocked every exit.

Only the Inca noblemen, the Orejones, remained calm in the face of impending annihilation. They formed a living wall around Atahualpa and fought with a desperation that impressed Pizarro as he hacked through plaited cane helmets and hide shields. He noticed that many of the warriors that fell to his sword had one or more limbs painted black as an outward sign of the death they had dealt in previous battles.

It wasn't long before the superiority of Toledo steel began to take its toll on the Orejones. Wooden swords did not even dent Spanish armor, while the conquistadors easily sliced through the cotton quilting that protected the pigeon breasted torsos of Atahualpa's guard. Finally, only three men stood between Pizarro and the golden litter. He cut down two of the Orejones with vicious blows that belied his advancing age and then glanced upward in triumph as he reached the circle of litter bearers.

Confronting his enemy at last, Atahualpa rose solemnly from his throne and stared fixedly into the conquistador's eyes. The boldness strangely faded from Pizarro's gaze, and the sword slipped from his fingers. The Inca king raised his arms heavenward in invocation. Then he untied the huge medallion from around his neck. It gleamed wickedly as he focused its rays upon the Spaniard's breastplate. In a moment a pool of molten steel appeared on the armor's surface, and the reek of sizzling flesh supplanted the stench of freshly-spilled Inca blood. Pizarro's scream pierced the din of battle as he slumped lifelessly to the ground. Blood trickling from his mouth, he froze in an attitude of repentance at the feet of the heathen king. The medallion flashed again and again as one by one the conquistadors discovered the awful secret of Atahualpa's power over men.

FAR AWAY SHE WAITS FOR ME

Far away she waits for me.
I feel her tentacles uncoiling,
reaching to pluck me
from my meteor ride.
Her eyes are embers.
Her tongue's a smoking brand.
I hear her stirring
on her bear trap bed.
She filing her teeth
& preparing her face
for treachery.

FETTERS AND CHAINS

Jason came from a very unloving family. Although he was an only child, his parents were usually too busy despising each other to pay him much mind. His most vivid childhood memories were of sullen faces, threatening fists, and constant bickering. It is no wonder, then, that at a very early age, Jason decided marriage was a trap to be avoided at all costs.

In accordance with this resolution, Jason spent his early teenage years, for the most part, avoiding the opposite sex. Sure there were moments when a hint of perfume or the curve of girlish hips would arouse in him that vague animal lust so peculiar to the pubescent male. But those lapses were always short-lived, for his built-in defense mechanism would soon conjure pinched images of his mother's owlish face so grotesque he would turn away from the object of his longing with disgust.

Strangely enough, it was this very aloofness that made Jason most appealing to those he sought to evade. Also, by the time he was seventeen, he had become so darkly handsome, with his flashing black eyes and chiseled features, that every girl in his class longed to be the one to unlock the mysterious brooding that possessed him.

At first, Jason was puzzled by the alluring glances of the girls who sized him up as he took his seat in history or English class. When the awful truth finally dawned on him, he reacted like all true masters of any game--he used his knowledge to conquer and destroy his opponent. Naturally, being so young, Jason saw these objectives in purely sexual terms.

So began a long string of girlfriends who he found, unwrapped, and unwound. If this description sounds a bit cold and formulaic, it was meant to be, for Jason developed a foolproof strategy of cold manipulation.

Invariably, each of Jason's encounters began when he permitted the female to make the first move. This gave his "prey" a false sense of security while, at the same time, making him appear vulnerable until he had gained a girl's complete trust. That usually didn't take long, considering his natural cunning and facility with the tender phrase. As one of the bereaved young ladies was to remark after his disappearance, "Jason could charm Cleopatra out of the arms of Anthony."

Another useful tactic Jason learned after two or three of these romances was to keep his woman off guard through a mixture of sweetness and cruelty. As a matter of fact, it seemed that a girl became hooked on him even sooner if he was lackadaisical about returning her phone calls or avoided her in the halls at school. It was also this same enigma that made it doubly hard for him to dispose of a lover once he had his way with her. Each abuse he heaped upon a girl always made her want him twice as badly. Little did she understand that his strained conversation and paleness were merely manifestations of the human animal balking from a trap.

Despite all the turmoil caused by his love life, Jason's senior year in high school went very well until a couple of weeks before the prom. At the time he was between girls and available. He had to decide which of the host of willing beauties should be given the privilege of taking him to the dance. He had narrowed it down to a pair of luscious juniors (who had been in hot pursuit for months) when the most peculiar thing occurred one morning before homeroom period.

As was his custom, Jason was strolling down the hall "taking inventory." He was so intent upon rating each girl he passed--noting her figure, face, and future possibilities--that it took him awhile to realize he, too, was under scrutiny.

Fearing that a teacher or the principal had guessed his game, he wheeled stiffly around, half expecting to discover a ferret-faced adult behind him. Instead, he found himself examining the shapeliest girl he had ever seen. Such a judgment was easy to make, considering she stood framed in a sunlit doorway which revealed every shadowy curve of her body through her dress. Ironically, the same dazzling glare that highlighted her figure, also masked her cocked face in a blinding aura of amber light.

As Jason noted every delicious inch of the girl's body, he became instantly aroused. He attempted to compliment her several times with his old line but found his throat so unnaturally constricted that he was unable to speak. Utterly disarmed by desire, he felt almost naked himself. In fact, he was so uncomfortable, he never questioned why such a dainty girl should wear a spiked chain bracelet more befitting the Hell's Angels than a high school co-ed.

At last, the girl shot Jason a dazzling smile. Numbly, he began babbling disjointed phrases that could have made no possible sense to anyone but her. When he walked dazedly away a few minutes later, even he could recall only that the girl's name was Hester and that he had asked her to the prom. Although he could not distinctly recall seeing her face, it's doubtful he could have resisted anyway.

On the night of the big dance, Jason was uncharacteristically apprehensive. He stayed locked in his bedroom all evening, adjusting his tux and fussing over his appearance. Finally, with the eighth chime of the hall clock ringing in his head, he stomped downstairs to hiss goodbye to his parents. He was especially uncivil to his mother when she dropped his date's corsage while snatching it from the refrigerator. His father's joke about him looking like a "stiff in a monkey suit" went over about as well. Oh, well. Who were they? Let them wallow in their ugly world.

Even behind the wheel of his old man's car, Jason couldn't relax. Nothing playing on the radio satisfied him, and he skipped from station to station. He wondered why he had not seen his date since that first morning. It seemed just plain unnatural that she hadn't phoned him or, at least, waited around for him after school. Was it possible that she actually planned to stand him up? How foolish he would look if he went to the biggest social event of the year with no lady hanging on his arm!

Only visions of Hester's sweet, shadowy body kept Jason from totally panicing as he turned onto Denison Street and headed toward the address the girl had given him during their only encounter. Could it be that she actually lived in such a ramshackle neighborhood? Had he not been so driven by lust, he certainly wouldn't have stayed to find out once he spied her soot-blackened apartment house dwarfed by the smokestacks of a nearby meat processing plant. As it was, he barely noticed the reek of old blood from the slaughterhouse next door when he boiled from his vehicle and charged up the front steps.

With his pulse thundering in his temples, Jason tapped lightly on the front door. Although it was a muggy May night, his teeth chattered and his eyes had a vague, glazed look about them. He was forced to rap more vigorously before he heard the clatter of high heels approaching from inside.

Finally, the door creaked open, and Jason was blinded by a blast-furnace-like flash of light. Only Hester's enticing voice told him he was indeed at the right address. He did not step inside, however, until her hot fingers closed about his own.

When the boy's eyes had adjusted to the glare, he found himself standing in a cavernous living room, the entire back wall of which was dominated by a fireplace. A mantle lined with hideous ebony curios ran the full length of this wall. Elsewhere about the chamber were scattered various pieces of furniture made of polished black oak. These glistened with such brillance, they appeared to generate their own light.

Jason's eyes eventually came to rest on Hester where she stood with the firelight dancing seductively on her face. Her own eyelids were coyly downcast. She was attired in a black, formal gown that sparkled with her every movement. Her plunging neckline attracted Jason like a thief is drawn to a strand of pearls. The sinister rattling of her spiked chain bracelet went totally undetected beneath the thudding of his heart.

Sensing her advantage, Hester ensnared Jason in her arms and led him in an enchanted waltz around the chamber. At that moment, as if on cue, soft music began to play. Jason was so bewitched by the sensual nature of this melody, he lost track of the course their dance followed across the living room and through an adjacent hallway. The next thing he knew, Hester had released her embrace, retreated a step, and slipped her dress off her shoulders and onto the floor. By now all thoughts of the prom had slipped from Jason's mind, as well.

Jason blinked in amazement as he drank in every slinky curve of the girl's naked form. At last, he realized that they were in a dimly-lit bedroom, and that she was motioning for him to lie back on the water bed behind him. When she saw that he was too numb to respond, she took his hand and ran it across the satin coverlet over the bed. This simple act brought him unspeakable pleasure and seemed to promise even more.

With the recklessness only carnal lust can produce, Jason tumbled backward and reached his hand for his lover. He hit the coverlet with a sploosh that made the gooseflesh thick on his buttocks. The next instant he felt himself sinking out of sight in a benumbing tank of dark liquid. He was completely out of breath by the time he touched the bottom, shoved off with one foot, and propelled himself to the surface. When he broke water, he was greeted by his first real glimpse of Hester's eyes.

A scream rattled from Jason's throat, and he sank from sight a second time. With the freezing water deadening his limbs, it felt like an eternity before he again hit bottom. When his foot finally did touch, a pair of jaws clamped shut around his ankle. Sharp teeth tore into his flesh, and a cloud of blood bubbled upward past his face. In an animal frenzy Jason kicked and thrashed until the lack of oxygen choked the fight out of him. Only as his tuxedo-clad form sagged to the bottom of the tank, did he see the bear trap that secured him.

Meanwhile, two crimson pupils peered expectantly downward into the dank pool. Just as the water quit bubbling, the faint buzz of a doorbell echoed from the hall. Hester glanced once more into the water to note a second trap and then pulled the satin coverlet in place over the bed frame. As she left the room, her hellish eyes were cast coyly downward. Her formal black gown sparkled with every delicious movement of her hips.

MARY AND EMMETT

Mary led her husband Emmett to the couch. She commanded him to sit in the condescending tone reserved for a pet. Mumbling vaguely to himself, the shriveled old man plopped onto the cushions and fixed his empty gaze on the television screen opposite him. The Jetsons were on, not that it really made much difference.

The old woman patted her husband on the shoulder and then trundled off into the adjoining kitchenette to wash the breakfast dishes. As she stacked the plates and coffee cups into the dishwasher, she glanced periodically at Emmett to make sure he hadn't toppled forward off the couch like he'd done so many times lately. How hard it was for her to believe that just a year ago the same man had planted a garden, mowed the lawn, and trimmed weeds from the doorstep of their old home. But that was before the arteries had begun to harden in his brain. Now, about all he could do was feed himself. The box of diapers beneath the kitchen table testified to that.

Mary's face clouded as she reflected upon the difficult period of adjustment she had had since moving into the Oakhurst Space Age Apartment Complex for the Elderly. Her husband's condition had worsened dramatically in that span of five months, which necessitated her babysitting him practically twenty-four hours a day. Also, that same proud independence that had prevented the woman from placing her husband in a nursing home, had also kept her, at first, from accepting such time-saving conveniences as dishwashers, intercoms, self-changing beds, and robot attendants with which her new home was fully equipped. Mary was still grumbling about these "gadgets" as she shoveled Emmett's half-eaten scrambled egg breakfast down the garbage disposal. At the same time, she couldn't help but marvel at the enormous capacity of those grinding disposal jaws that had once made short work of a giant, economy size bottle of detergent that had slipped from her grasp. She would never forget how the crunch of plastic, that had followed its plummet down the drain, had made her skin crawl.

A buzzer sounded above the old woman's head, and she tilted her wizened face toward the ceiling.

"Yes."

"Do. . .you. . .need. . .anything. . .at. . .the. . . supermarket. . .to-day. . .Mrs. Gray?" droned a mechanical voice from a concealed speaker.

"No thank you."

"You. . .are. . .welcome."

Another buzzer sounded, and Mary opened the dishwasher to find her plates and cups all sparkling clean. She soon became so absorbed in restacking them in the cupboard that she didn't notice Emmett get to his feet and tiptoe across the carpet, his face beaming like a mischievous child. At that moment an exhaust fan switched on automatically to clear the air of steam rising from her dishes. Its steady roar completely concealed the closing of the front door. It was another ten minutes before Mary turned from cleaning the kitchen sink to find the sofa empty.

"Emmett? You know I hate playing hide-and-seek. Come out, come out wherever you are!"

As expected, there was no reply, so the old woman went through her daily ritual of checking behind the couch, in the closets, and under the beds. Emmett was not to be found in any of those hiding places, but Mary was still unconcerned. With a triumphant smile she charged into the bathroom and flung open the shower curtain. When she found the stall empty, she hastened into the living room and pressed the intercom buzzer.

"Emmett's escaped again!" she shouted into the contraption. "You'll need to go fetch him."

"Yes. . .Mrs. Gray."

For half-an-hour Mary paced nervously back and forth across the carpet, biting her fingernails to the quick. Finally, there was a knock on the door, and two robot attendants ushered Emmett into the living room. The old man glanced warily from one of his captors to the other. He mumbled incoherently until his wife stepped forward and took him firmly by the ear.

"You're a bad boy," scolded Mary. "Look at all the trouble you've caused these. . .er. . ."

Mary paused uncertainly as she regarded the humanoid figures that towered over her. Dressed in their bright blue uniforms, they would have almost passed for real security guards if it had not been for their clear, plastic, dome-like heads.

"May. . .I. . .suggest. . .that. . .you. . .keep. . .your. . . door. . .locked," droned the first robot while he bowed from the room.

"May. . .I. . .suggest. . .that. . .you. . .keep. . .your. . . door. . .locked," repeated the other bubblehead when he closed the door.

"May. . .I. . .suggest. . .that. . .you. . .mind. . .your. . . own. . .business," mocked the old woman, hooking the security chain behind them. "Come on, Emmett, it's time for your morning shave."

Mary retained her firm grip on Emmett's ear and led him into the bathroom. She had just removed his undershirt and lathered up his face when a buzzer announced another visitor. With a curse, she stormed into the foyer and ripped open the front door to find the robot postman waiting with the morning mail. She had little time to examine it, however, before the garbled strains of "Mary Had a Little Lamb" had her scurrying for the bathroom. When she peeped breathlessly inside, there was Emmett, still dressed in his pants and best shoes, splashing and laughing in the shower. Naturally, he had forgotten to draw the plastic curtain, and the automatic drain strained with a deafening screech to channel off the water gushing onto the title floor. By the time Mary had retrieved Emmett from the shower, had shaved him, and had set him to work with a mop, the old wife was soaked and on the verge of tears.

The mid-afternoon sun filtered through the drawn living room curtains, highlighting the paleness of Mary's cheeks. The old woman rested in an overstuffed chair with a damp rag plastered on her forehead. The apartment was much too stuffy for her liking, but it seemed to have an anesthetizing effect on Emmett, who was stretched out dozing on the couch. Mary became oblivious to the heat watching her husband's toothless mouth form little o's of snoring. Soon her head slouched forward on her chest, and she was sound asleep.

When Mary awoke, the room was completely dark. Although she could no longer hear or see Emmett, it wasn't hard for her to pinpoint his position by the faint but distinct odor that wafted across the room. Mary flicked on the lamp beside her chair and was greeted by a disgusting sight. There lay her husband face-up on the sofa hugging a pillow and sucking his thumb. He must have gotten too warm during his sleep, for now his trousers dangled from one leg onto the floor. His diaper had been ripped open, and telltale custard-color stains covered the cushions beneath him. There were similar stains smeared on the tails of his white shirt.

"Emmett Gray! Wake up this instant!"

The old man jerked awake, and a custard-colored hand appeared from beneath him to wipe the sleep from his eyes. With a shriek Mary leaped forward and took Emmett by the ear. She jerked him to his feet and led him kicking and bawling into the bathroom. There he tripped on the trousers that still dangled from one leg and fell with a splat on the padded floor of the shower stall. Mary drew the plastic curtain and turned on the shower full blast. Emmett sputtered as a sheet of cold water hit him square in the face.

"You lather up good, you hear!" hissed Mary as she tossed the old man a bar of soap. "I'm going to get you a clean change of clothes, so don't you dare leave this bathroom."

Mary returned moments later and commanded her husband to strip. While he handed his shirt and pants through the shower curtain, a faint odor made the old woman gag. She turned, holding her breath, and stuffed the vile garments through the clothes chute near the sink. For once she was thankful that the robot laundry did all of her washing.

When Emmett was showered and freshly dressed, Mary led him by the hand to the miniature table that divided the living room from the kitchenette. Then she sat him down and went to fetch some eggs and bacon from the refrigerator. In a matter of minutes she whipped up a fluffy omelet that she heaped onto Emmett's plate. With thoughts of shampooing the sofa clouding her face, Mary finally collapsed opposite her husband to watch him eat.

Emmett sank his fork into the steaming platter of eggs but did not lift it to his mouth. He was plain sick of eggs. That was about all that lady ever fixed him. Making choo-choo noises, he dug a tunnel through the center of the omelet instead.

Mary reached across the table and gave the old man a light slap on the hand. "Don't play with your food," she snapped.

Like a spoiled child, Emmett threw down his fork and then hurled his plate onto the floor. Instantly, Mary jumped to her feet and aimed a blow at her husband's head. At the last second her clenched fist veered past his ear and came thudding down on the table.

"Look at all the food you've wasted!" howled Mary, nursing her bruised hand. "And look at that mess! Now, I'm going to have to feed your whole meal to the garbage disposal. Now--"

Suddenly, a malicious smile flickered across Mary's lips as she envisioned that giant, economy size bottle of detergent disappearing down the drain. She turned to flip on the exhaust fan. When she once more faced her husband, all the thunder had faded from her brow.

"Come over here to the sink, Emmett," she cooed below the roar of the fan. "There's something over here you can play with. . ."

FEAR LURKED IN THE SHADOWS HERE

The old mill was crisscrossed with vines,
and part of the wall had collapsed
in the last windstorm.
Inside, doorways gaped
like gaps in a diseased gum line.
Pipes dripped and bats squeaked.
The wind sighed through an air vent
like an orphaned spook.
Fear lurked in the shadows here,
bristling the mange
of stray dogs and vagrants.

THE PRICE OF A PINT

The hobo rubbed his arms and muttered incoherently as he glanced toward a trash bin overflowing with greasy newspapers and broken cardboard boxes. Even if he bedded down there again tonight, he'd probably freeze to death. Man, this was the coldest November ever! According to the flashing sign outside the Tenth Avenue Bank, it was already one degree below zero at six p.m. What he really needed was a little "antifreeze" to brace himself against the cold.

But how was he, Raymond Bartholomew, to afford such a luxury as the price of a pint? With heating bills on the rise, people just weren't as generous as they'd been last summer. Lately, a whole week's panhandling barely netted enough for an occasional cup of coffee. Even worse, business was so slow in most restaurants that they weren't hiring extra dishwashers. Without that money, he'd even lost his bed at the flophouse.

Raymond began to pace furiously back and forth across the alley he now called home. His face was a blur of tangled whiskers, and his hair protruded wildly from beneath a clownish bowler hat. His once fashionable suit was stained and tattered. With the layers of grime caked on his skin, he looked vaguely Negroid lurking in the shadows.

There was always the possibility of a discrete mugging or two to keep a fellow going, but Raymond was much too squeamish for that. Besides, the only people weak enough for him to handle were either school children or senior citizens. Over the years he'd dealt with too many such individuals to find harming them very palatable.

Raymond dug his freezing hands deep into his pockets and wandered out onto Tenth Avenue. As he stumbled past a row of dark store fronts, he stared through their barred windows at the same type of warm overcoats and luxurious sweaters that had once hung in his own closet. Finally, he came to a halt in front of Falcon Brothers' Liquors. It was the only place on the block that was still open, and the warm lights glowed inside like an expensive whiskey in the bottom of a crystal tumbler.

The hobo opened the front door and slipped into the shop. Casually, he examined several shelves of gift liquors in colored bottles while casing the joint. The proprietor, a burly bare-armed man, had risen when he came in and was now studying him in the ceiling mirror just overhead.

Raymond sidled around a display of dinner wines and proceeded up the brandy aisle. Glancing into the mirror, he saw that his every movement was being logged by the big hulk behind the cash register. Oh well, if he couldn't swipe a pint, at least he was going to take his time and get warm!

Raymond spent a good ten minutes peering at the various brands and flavors of brandy--a liquor of which he had at one time been a connoisseur. When his hands finally began to thaw, he reached out to "inspect" a preferred bottle more closely. His fingers no sooner closed around it than a heavy paw thumped down on his shoulder.

"May I help you?" growled a voice close to his ear.

"Just looking," Raymond replied with a twitching smile. "I see you have my favorite brandy in stock."

"Gee, am I ever relieved to hear that. Would you like to <u>buy</u> a bottle to take with you?"

"Uh. . .Yes, I would, but. . .unfortunately I forgot my wallet at home."

"Yeah, I know. And your broker's out of town, too, right?"

Rough hands seized Raymond by the collar and the seat of the pants, and he was given the bum's rush out into the street. He skipped nimbly across the sidewalk until crashing headlong into a trash barrel set out along the curb. When he came to moments later, he found himself sprawled in the gutter covered with coffee grounds and rotted fruit.

Not bothering to brush himself off, Raymond got to his feet and weaved drunkenly back to the liquor store. Damn! His assailant hadn't even waited to see how much damage he had done. He was back behind the cash register reading a girly magazine.

Raymond staggered away from the door and started down the block. His vision was blurry, and his lips felt swollen. What was he to do?

Wiping the corner of his mouth, he came away with his palm smeared with blood. "God, and all along I thought I was slobbering on myself again," he muttered. "What a waste of good blood. What a. . .Hey! That's it! That's It!"

Raymond quickened his pace as he entered a dingy neighborhood comprised mainly of tenement houses. This was the dark side of the city unlit by streetlights or the hope of salvation. Only the most desperate sort of white men dared venture here, and Bartholomew cringed as shadows flitted past him reeking of day-old whiskey and vomit cologne. Several times he heard shrieks emit from the bowels of an adjacent alley. Then he understood why people turned their heads and walked away from daylight stabbings.

Three blocks into the darkness, the hobo came to a low professional-looking building illuminated by a single bulb over the doorway. He pressed the buzzer, and a nurse appeared on the other side of a barred window. She peered cautiously past him into the street. Seeing he was alone, she opened the door latch electronically and motioned for him to enter.

Raymond found himself in the shadowy anteroom of Roma Corporation, one of a dozen metro companies in the business of buying and selling blood. The need for such companies always existed in a city of two million people, for there were never enough donors to meet the needs of a diseased population prone to violent accident and heinous crime. What is more, Roma and its counterparts weren't too particular about the type of scabrous lowlife from which they obtained their blood supply. Filling the quota was always the bottom line. If they had to set up headquarters in the middle of a ghetto, so be it.

The same nurse who had admitted Raymond to the premises emerged from behind a hospital screen and took a seat at a dented metal desk. Producing an official-looking form, she nodded toward a chair on the other side of the room. Her movements were brisk, and her eyes about as sympathetic as flint. When Raymond was seated, she snapped, "Name?"

"Raymond Bartholomew."

"Address?"

"Uh. . .Tenth Avenue."

"Have you given any blood in the past month?"

"No."

"Are you presently taking any medication?"

"No."

"Have you been out of the country recently?"

"No."

"Do you have hepatitis, syphilis, AIDS, or any other communicable disease?"

"No."

"Have you drunk any alcoholic beverages in the past week?"

"No."

"Okay, put your mark here and go down the hall to your right."

"Wait a minute," said Raymond coldly. "I'm very capable of signing my name."

"Then sign here."

"Before I do, I'd like to know what this is for."

"It's a simple release," droned the nurse. "Now, will you hurry up. I haven't got all night!"

Bartholomew approached the desk, snatched up a pen, and scribbled his signature. During the entire interview, the nurse hadn't looked at him once.

"Before I go through with this, how much am I going to get paid?"

"Between thirty and forty dollars. It depends on your blood type. Now, will you make up your mind!"

Swallowing hard, Raymond nodded his assent and then passed along a darkened corridor and through a pair of swinging doors. He emerged into a large, well-lit room furnished almost exclusively with rows of padded tables. Several of these were occupied by elderly residents of the ghetto. Oh well, Raymond thought as he glanced around, at least I should get top dollar for my Type O blood.

An ugly black nurse approached Raymond and led him to the nearest table. She instructed him to take off his coat, roll up his sleeve, and lie down. She scurried over to a medicine cabinet, returning momentarily with a needle, hose, tourniquet, plastic sack, and a bottle of rubbing alcohol. She wrapped the tourniquet around Raymond's arm and gave it a couple of twists. Then, without warning, she sterilized a spot on his forearm and rammed the needle home. Before he could even yelp, she withdrew and reburied it a second time. She tried three more times to hit a vein before finally calling out in frustration to an elderly nurse. By that time, her patient had become strangely pale beneath the coat of grime on his face.

A testy white woman stormed over to Raymond's table and jerked the needle from the other nurse's hand. "Why can't they send me anyone but student nurses?" she raged as she successfully tapped a vein with one vicious poke of the needle. At that moment Raymond must have lost consciousness, for later he couldn't remember watching them hook up the plastic sack into which his blood was dripping.

Bartholomew closed his eyes, but the nightmare didn't go away. No matter how many liquor bottles he conjured in his mind, he couldn't blot out the stale smell of urine wafting from the black fellow next to him.

God, how unfair life can be, reflected Raymond. To look at me now, who would ever believe that only last fall, I was the one examining patients on padded tables? Somehow, washing dishes isn't very satisfying after twelve years of college, medical school, and specialized training in pediatrics. Nor is being a social outcast, for that matter. . .

But how else was I to examine the girl for VD? Of course, I should have never agreed to treat her without first notifying her parents. That was stupid! Yet, when you deliver a child into the world and see her through the measles, mumps, and chicken pox, you do feel a certain responsibility toward her. I guess I should have been less concerned about her embarrassment and more concerned with my own reputation.

Still I can't see how anyone could get sexual satisfaction from a simple medical examination, as she later claimed. A little rich girl might say anything, though, to keep from losing her allowance. Why should she care that I got expelled from the A.M.A. for sexually deviant behavior with a minor and would never practice medicine again?

The other patient began to moan softly, and Raymond peeked in his direction. The old Negro was gripping his arm just above where the needle protruded from it. His black skin shimmering with sweat, he reminded Raymond of a stereotypical slave from one of those second-rate Civil War movies. The only difference was that his master, the ghetto, hadn't needed any whips or chains to inflict the required amount of suffering.

Bartholomew studied the needle protruding from his own arm. I still must be in shock, he reasoned. Otherwise, wouldn't I feel some kind of pain? Isn't it funny how many times I took blood samples without once considering how frightening it was for the patient? Oh well, at least tonight I'll be able to return to the liquor store and buy two pints of brandy! Won't that clerk be surprised to see me back again? Maybe the SOB will even apologize when I flash a little green. Then I'll get a hotel room and sleep until noon. Under real sheets. And won't a nice hot bath feel good? And a shave. Why, I'll even be able to get my suit cleaned and pressed! Then I'll look like a proper--

"Hey, mista! You! Hey!"

Raymond woke with a start and discovered his ugly black nurse hovering over him. She was tapping his shoulder impatiently while glancing at her watch.

"Yo time's up," she muttered, "and you ain't gonna git paid."

"Excuse me?"

"Look at yo sack, mista. You ain't but half filled it with blood. Didn't they tell you we only pays for a full unit?"

"You mean if I don't give a whole pint, I don't get any money?"

"That's right! Looks like we's just gonna have to pack it back in ya."

"Pack what back in me?"

"Yo blood. Now, you lay back an' be still. This is

gonna hurt some."

The nurse raised the plastic sack even with her head, and blood began flowing back down the long tube. The hobo winced and grabbed his arm. This time shock did little to dull the pain. When the sack was empty, the nurse yanked the needle free and slapped a band-aid over the hole. Pointing to a side exit, she said, "Okay, you can go."

"Go?"

"Are you deaf besides bein' a po bleeda? I said git outta here!"

Suddenly, Raymond felt very angry. He had gone through a lot for the price of a pint, and he wasn't going to be cheated. Brushing aside the nurse, he rushed over to a cart loaded with fresh blood. Before the staff could recover, he tore open a container and chugged it in a single gulp.

By the time Bartholomew had finished his second bottle, the entire room was in an uproar. Student nurses were screaming. Buzzers were ringing. Patients were bellowing. One old black man became so frightened, he dove under a table, dislodging the needle from his arm. In seconds, the floor was flooded with blood squirting from the plastic sack.

The head nurse came rushing through the swinging doors in response to the alarm bell. Spotting Raymond, she wasted no time. With a grunt, she hurled herself at him, planting her fingernails in the middle of his back. Bartholomew shrugged her off as if she were an opinion with which he disagreed. There was a strange gleam in his eye. His mouth was rimmed with crimson. With a single bound, he hurdled the table between him and the side exit. In another, he was out the door. Tenth Avenue was soon to become a very unsafe place for weak, warm-blooded beings.

THE REVENGE OF OLD MAN MOONEY

Old man Mooney was a mean old fart. After he retired from his job at the glue factory downtown, he spent most of his time makin' life miserable fer me an' my brother Billie. He lived by hisself two doors up from us in this big old shacky blue house. The way he guarded the place, though, you'da thought it belonged to Rockefeller, or somethin'. Cripe, if anyone set foot in his yard, Mooney was all over 'im like flies on a squished toad.

Of course, us kids never yanked the old man's chain, or nothin'. Not much! He had a real neat vineyard an' apple orchard in his backyard that was always loaded with ripe fruit durin' the summer. After dark we'd sneak over there an' gorge ourselves 'til we jess about puked. At first, he musta thought the birds was scarfin' his grapes 'cause he put up this big ol' scarecrow. He got wise in the end, though. Cripe, I'll never forget the night he stood there in the scarecrow's place. I almost had a bird when he grabbed me on m' way home. He'da caught me, too, if my arm hadn'ta been so covered with grape slime that he lost his grip.

What really started the feud goin' 'tween us an'

old man Mooney was when he found a hoof print in his garden an' blamed me an' Billie of kifin' his lettuce. We was really innocent that time, even if our folks wouldn't believe us. Heck, Pa whooped us so hard with his razor strap that we just had to get even with the old fart that got us in Dutch. We'da done it, too, the very next day, if old man Mooney hadn't chased us off before we was finished splatterin' his house with mud balls. Boy, when Pa found out, we got pounded even harder than the first time!

Of course, a coupla thrashin's wasn't gonna discourage me an' Billie too much, 'specially with Halloween comin' up. We laid low fer a while, though, an' plotted our strategy real careful like. When the night fer trick or treatin' finally come, we charged over to old man Mooney's right off. We figgered we'd hit him while the most kids was at his front door beggin' candy. There was only one hitch to our plan. No one went to his house 'cause the cheap old buzzard had all the lights off!

Anyhow, we kinda slunk around in the dark fer a while jumpier than two toads on a hot plate while we got out the stockin's we "borrowed" from Ma an' pulled 'em down over our faces. Don't get me wrong. We wasn't gonna rob the place, or nothin'. We jess wanted to wax his windows good fer him. 'Bout the time I got out my candle an' started smearin' up a big old bay window, this light comes on inside the house. There was Mooney's fat, gray face not two inches from mine!

I gave a little gasp an' run smack into my brother Billie, knockin' both of us flat. We was up in a pig's wink, though, our feet justa spinnin' an' throwin' mud an' clumps of grass. We could still hear old man Mooney cussin' us by name as we jumped the fence an' cut out fer home. It seems our masks hadn't fooled him a lick.

It wasn't long after that that old man Mooney kicked off. To tell ya the truth, we'da been real glad it happened if Pa hadn'ta forced us to go to the funeral with the rest of the neighborhood. It was gonna be held at Mooney's house, an', cripe, who knows what could happen once we was there! He swore he'd get us fer what we done to his place. Maybe he still would. Not that we believed in hoodoo, or nothin', ya understand.

The day of the funeral was a total pain, let me tell ya. First, Ma got me an' Billie up at the crack of dawn an' hurried us through breakfast like we was in stinkin' reform school, or somethin'. Then she made us take a bath <u>in the middle of week!</u> An' did she get steamed when I forgot to wash my neck. Shoot, it was an honest mistake that anyone coulda made. Yet, she scrubbed me 'til I got an Injun sunburn that didn't go away fer three days. Then she squawked 'til I put on my new hand-me-down suit. The dang coat is so small that I can't breathe right when it's buttoned. I can't move real good in it, neither, the way the sleeves creep up to my elbows. I don't know who was stiffer, me or old man Mooney, by the time the whole shebang was over!

As I was sayin' before, the funeral was held over at Mooney's place. We arrived 'round noon, an' though me an' Billie's 'bout as Catholic as frog spit, we crossed ourselves three or four times before we dared go inside. Our pa's threats of a whoopin' kinda helped build up our courage some, too.

Cripe, no wonder old man Mooney was always spyin' out his windows. There sure weren't much to look at inside the house! A coupla old horsehair chairs was 'bout all the furniture he had. The walls was bare, too. There weren't no pitchers, no book shelves, or even a mirror. After glancin' 'round, I was kinda glad this was the first time we ever visited him, proper-like.

In the middle of the livin' room, of all places, the

undertaker had set up a coupla sawhorses an' slapped Mooney's coffin right on top of 'em. The coffin wasn't much more than an old pine box with brass handles, an' me an' Billie scoped it out real good before Pa was able to prod us forward to "pay our respects."

At first, we couldn't believe it was old man Mooney who was stuffed in that box. There was actually a <u>smile</u> on his face. The undertaker musta wired his fat, old cheeks to get him to grin that way. However that grin got there, we was spooked enough by it to cross the livin' room an' set down as far from that coffin as we could. You can bet we made dang sure we was close to the front door, too. If old man Mooney set up, or somethin', we wanted to make a clean getaway, let me tell ya.

Finally, after everyone had a chance to mill around fer a bit, Preacher Rowe started what Ma called the "eulogy." It was 'bout that same time that me an' Billie begun noticin' a powerful bad smell. Cripe, the more the preacher rambled on, the stronger that smell seemed to get. It was kinda a cross 'tween dead carp an' cow crap. Pretty soon, even old Rowe had to stop an' "catch his breath." By then, everyone was too green to pay him much mind anyhow.

Billie, meanwhile, kept makin' these little burpin' noises. I never recognized what they was 'til he barfed all over my new hand-me-down suit, clean neck, an' all. Cripe, you'da thought someone let a bag fulla rattlers loose in the room, the way the folks scattered.

After the place cleared out, the undertaker located the source of the smell right off. It was old man Mooney "splittin' the cheese." They had to cork him up before the funeral could go on. No wonder he had that grin plastered on his face. He'd gotten his revenge without resortin' to no hoodoo. Me an' Billie can sure testify to that!

HISS N' SPIT

Lounging on the sofa back,
she soaks up the sun,
her eyes yellow slits of fire.
From her perch she insolently
surveys the room
with a cool turn of her head.
She grooms her regal fur
with a barbed tongue
that's equally adept
at flaying flesh from bone.
The aquarium holds
her hors-d'oeuvres,
the bird cage her main course.
In Hiss N' Spit's house
the humans were
neutered and declawed.

THE BUD MONSTER

Had I known what was to follow, I never would have agreed to feed the Fraiser's cat while they were on vacation. Yet, what could I do? Gossip had it that my next door neighbor's marriage was in trouble. When they told me how their trip to Myrtle Beach was to be a second honeymoon, I felt compelled to oblige. Although I've lived alone for over twenty years since my dear Eloise passed away, I guess I'm still a sucker for romance.

I'd seen their sneaky cat stalking baby rabbits in the backyard, and it had sickened me to watch her tear a cuddly bunny to shreds. I must grudgingly admit she was a pretty creature, though, with greenish-yellow eyes and a decorative white patch on her neck and chest.

"We call her Bud," said my neighbor's wife with a flirtatious wink, "because she absolutely loves people."

"Yeah, her name is short for Buddy," added Mr. Fraiser. "You'll have to be careful, though, or she'll take advantage of you. Especially be sure to ration her food. She'll chow down the whole bag if you let her."

"I can tell she's an eater," I replied. "I swear she's the largest house cat I've ever seen."

"And could you do one more thing for us? Pretty please."

"What's that, Mrs. Fraiser?"

"Could you shoo the cat away from the road if you see her out there? You know how dangerous the traffic can get on Highway 5."

"Now, don't you worry about. . .Bud. I'll take good care of her. Just go and enjoy your stay at the ocean."

That evening I heaped the cat's plastic bowl with fish-shaped dry food and set it on my back steps like I had promised. The bowl no sooner left my hand than the huge tabby fur ball came bounding from the neighbor's shrubs to pounce on the feast like a miniature lion. I chuckled as I watched her feed greedily and then laughed aloud when she abandoned her empty dish to rub contentedly against my legs.

"What an appetite you have!" I scolded. "You eat more than two cats!"

Then I made the mistake of picking up Bud to stroke her fur and gibber nonsense to her. She clung to me in total adoration, snagging her claws in my best sweater. When I set her down, I had the hardest time pushing her away so I could get inside my screen door.

With her owners gone for a week, Bud decided to adopt me. Every morning I found her waiting on my back stoop when I went out to buy a newspaper. And in the evening, there she was again. As soon as my Ford pulled in the driveway from my daily trip to the Senior

Center, Bud would streak mewing to greet me. She rubbed against my legs and got under my feet every time I crawled out of the car. Sometimes she even leaped in my lap if I didn't slide out from under the steering wheel quickly enough. Then she tried to follow me in the house. I had the hardest time holding her off with one leg while I slid sideways through the door. I had no rest even then because the crazy cat whined and whined until I came out with her supper dish loaded with food.

After a few days, I was so sick of Bud's unwanted attention that I seriously considered checking into a motel until the dang feline's owners returned from Myrtle Beach. Unfortunately, even that didn't solve the problem because the Fraisers split up soon after their honeymoon vacation. I'm not the nosy type, so I don't know the particulars. I did, however, notice that one evening there was plenty of screaming over at their place followed by a visit from the local police. Before it was all over, my neighbor's wife boiled out of the house and slammed a couple suitcases in the trunk of her red Corvette. "So what if I do have lots of male friends?" I heard her bellow. Then she sped off, never to return.

Mr. Fraiser wasn't home much after that. His lawn went unmowed and his cat unfed often for weeks at a time. That made Bud an even more permanent fixture on my back stoop. Now, what was I to do? I was renting my house, and the landlord, who owned three beautiful Persian cats himself, disapproved of his

89

tenants having pets.

"Animals make too much of a mess," he had said the day before when he stopped to pick up the rent and saw how Bud rubbed against my legs while he and I chatted in the driveway. "I can't allow my renters to have pets, or I'd have to replace the carpet every time someone moved out. I'd never make any money on this place."

After I had lied about only watching Bud temporarily, I worried all night that my landlord would kick me out if he learned how much time the cat really spent at the house. He lived two doors up the road, so it wouldn't be very difficult for him to spy on me. I was only paying $200 a month, which stretched my pension as it was. But even though I would be in a world of trouble if I had to move elsewhere, I still found it difficult to be mean to an abandoned animal. I just wished her demonstrations of love for me weren't so obnoxious and obsessive.

I guess I'm just an old softy because the very next afternoon I let Bud come in out of the weather during a terrible thunderstorm. That was another big mistake. She immediately made herself at home, peeking behind the couch and into cupboards and closets. Even worse, she followed me around like a Seeing Eye dog. She loved to scoot through my legs and remained so close underfoot that she kept tripping me. I couldn't even go to the bathroom without her tagging along.

She became such a pest that I went to the refrigerator and cut her a piece of cheese. After dangling it in front of her nose, I led her to the back door and chucked her treat outside. Off she shot to pounce on the delicious morsel in total disregard of the drenching downpour.

"Tricked by your own greed, you crazy cat," I shouted after her. "See if you come in this house again."

But come in again she did! My arthritic, old bones could never slam the door fast enough whenever she'd ambush me on my return from the fitness walks Dr. Weinstein prescribed for my heart condition. All I wanted to do then was shed my sweaty jogging suit and crawl into a nice tub of hot water. Instead, I had to play hide-and-seek with Bud, who scooted in the house before me to disappear beneath the bed or behind the entertainment center where she wrapped herself in stereo wires and TV cords.

Yep, Bud had a habit of appearing at the most inopportune time, all right. Whenever I came home from shopping and had to lug heavy sacks of canned goods up the back steps, there she'd be right beneath my feet tripping me up. Then she'd streak into the kitchen to swish her tail contentedly while I cursed her tabby hide under my breath. Of course, she had to poke her nose in every grocery sack to see what was inside. If I didn't watch her carefully, every time she ended up with the fish sandwich I bought at the deli. Once she even jumped onto the kitchen counter and knocked a jar of pickles onto the floor. The jar smashed into a million little pieces that I kept stepping on and embedding in my feet for months afterward!

One day after Bud almost upended me down the cellar staircase, I punted her like a hairy football off the porch. She hit the ground hard and then dove into my neighbor's untrimmed hedge to sulk and hiss. She didn't come around for a couple of days after that until hunger got the better of her. Then she was back mewing, mewing, mewing over The Price Is Right until I finally broke down and let her in. She naturally showed her appreciation by sharpening her claws on my new recliner and getting muddy footprints on a freshly-washed bedspread. When I bent to swat her on the head, she hissed so menacingly that I resorted to the treat-out-the-back-door-trick to finally get her to leave.

Bud's sudden viciousness shook me up so much that my pulse rate jumped way out of control. As I gobbled down a glycerin pill, I seriously began thinking of ways to rid myself of that greedy, green-eyed beast forever! What if I lured her into the car with some catnip and then dropped her off in a neighboring town? How about giving her to the SPCA? Or maybe I could borrow my brother's German shepherd to chase her away. Of course, that might get me evicted if Bruno tore into my landlord's cats, too! They sometimes came over to play with Bud although they were too skiddish to ever approach the house.

As I continued to consider my options, Bud again began mewing furiously on the back stoop. Gritting my teeth, I went into the kitchen and busied myself with a sinkful of dishes that I should have washed days ago. I had just begun scouring the pans when I heard the cat banging against the front door. Her fit intensified into a frenzy until she became impossible to ignore. Finally, she came and sat with her back to me just outside the kitchen window where she couldn't help but be noticed. I could tell by her posture that she was angry. My dear Eloise used to get her back up the same way whenever she thought I wasn't paying her enough attention.

If I'd have been a crueler man, I would have spiked that cat's food with rat poison long ago. Instead, I went to the door and let Bud in. She immediately began circling my legs and rubbing against me until I picked her up and stroked her fur. "You're creepy and kooky and altogether ooky," I sighed. "What am I going to do with you?"

I set the cat on the floor and began cuffing her playfully. Then I teased her with a piece of cheese. Every time she sprang to grab it, I pulled it just out of her reach before offering it again. Finally, Bud leaped up and planted her fangs deep into my wrist. Blood oozed from my punctured skin, and I yelped in surprise. This time the cat did not follow me when I made a beeline into the bathroom to pour peroxide on the wound. I had heard of people getting cat scratch fever, and I wasn't going to be one of them. After wrapping several layers of gauze over my wrist, I made up my mind once and for all to rid myself of that vicious beast!

I grabbed a broom from the closet and rushed into the kitchen. I expected to find the cat cowering in a corner or whining defensively near the door. Instead, she leaped on my shoulder from atop the refrigerator, slashing wildly with her claws. I felt a searing pain in my left eye and toppled backward onto the table, smashing it into kindling. The monster continued to slash my eyes until both pupils were rendered useless. Then she leaped aside, hissing and snarling like a thing possessed, while I punched blindly at thin air.

Finally adrenalin kicked in, and I leaped to my feet like a Senior Olympian. I careened across the kitchen, groped through the living room, and ripped open the front door. With Bud's horrific caterwauling still ringing in my ears, I leaped off what I remembered to be the porch. Afterward, I bolted into total darkness toward the roar of traffic on Highway 5. I'm sure the driver that hit me had no time to stop. I only wanted away from the Bud monster, no matter what the cost!

Now, I lie in the hospital with my blind eyes bandaged and my broken legs in traction. In an effort to console me, the nurse says it's a beautiful, sunny day. She also says she has a special surprise that involves a visit from my landlord and a furry friend.

"What do you mean by f-f-furry friend?" I stuttered aghast.

"Why your cute, cuddly cat. Your landlord has

been taking care of it for you, and he plans to bring it over during visiting hours. He didn't have the heart to send it to the SPCA after all you've been through. We normally don't allow animals in the hospital, Mr. White, but we thought we'd make an exception this time. Now, doesn't that make you feel better?"

THE GOLDENROD

Jacob Martin cut loose a vile string of epitaphs as he struck out at a flight of bees that dive-bombed him from his blind side. It was swelteringly hot for the twenty-third of September, and the afternoon sun glinted from the row of red lumps that sprouted on the paunchy man's bald head. When he shifted the scythe from one sweaty paw to the other, the fresh bee stings made him wince with pain.

The fat man stared across the yard and swore again. He was standing chest-deep in a sea of goldenrod that sprouted from the earth where his once bountiful garden had flourished. A continuous gaudy wave of weeds now stretched from the very steps of his back porch to the distant hills aglow with crimson oaks. This was the third time in as many weeks that he had been forced to hew a new path to his dog kennel that lie in the center of his backyard. The very thought of this annoyance threw Martin into another sudden fit of labor. With an anger oblivious to heat or pain, he hacked away at the arrow-straight stalks that hemmed him in. Ironically, the scythe was the only one of his gardening tools that wasn't caked with rust.

Half-an-hour later, an exhausted Jacob Martin chased off another swarm of attacking bees and then unlocked the dog pen to collapse inside. He lay panting facedown in the dirt until old Duke, his prize beagle, waddled from the kennel to lick the sides of his flushed cheeks. Jacob dazedly rolled over on his back and threw his arms around the hound. Outside the steel mesh enclosure, a shudder passed through the goldenrod. Saw-edged leaves wigwagged silent messages. Waving plumes of flower heads, heavy with insects, bent toward the pen as if in an attitude of listening. What resulted was the same faint rustling buzz that had kept the man sleeplessly tossing night after night in his bed. He recognized it instantly and huddled even closer to Duke. Strangely, there wasn't even a whisper of a breeze.

Jacob could feel the sun burn through his tightly closed eyelids as he pondered with growing fear an enigma that had haunted him since early spring. What still totally mystified him was the amazing regenerative powers of the goldenrod army that had invaded his property. He knew from research in the town library that the scientific name for the goldenrod was Solidago from the Latin "solidare," meaning to make whole. The plants were so-called because of their reputed curative powers. Until they had grown to five-foot in height in a week's time, he had always assumed that these curative powers referred to their potential benefit to the human species.

The only human in whom Jacob had dared confide this enigma was his neighbor, Aaron Shotts. Aaron was another gardening fanatic and had watched with alarm as the goldenrod spread in an almost calculated series of maneuvers from the foot of the distant hills to subjugate first his potato patch and then his prize-winning rose garden. Consequently, he had gladly joined forces with Jacob that spring for a counterattack against the Solidago.

Jacob shook his head in wonderment while recalling the neighbors' attempt to annihilate their adversary. They had used a pesticide that he had never known to fail even on the most resistant strain of dandelion, and predictably the treated weeds shriveled and died. There was little time for celebration, however, for within a month a hardier army of goldenrod had sprung up to reclaim the garden plots. Upon its resurgence, the old men were shocked to learn that it now thrived upon the very pesticides that had previously choked it out. Some of the plants sprang up to six-foot in height. More shocking still, the bees also grew to gigantic proportions. The droning of these insects continued twenty-four hours a day as they feasted gluttonously upon their hosts.

Suddenly, old Duke stiffened. The rustling of the goldenrod increased to a deafening level, but somehow the sound went undetected by the man huddled beside him. The hairs bristled on the hound's back, and he growled a low warning before disappearing tail-first into his kennel. Despite his master's repeated coaxing, the dog remained cowering within.

Finally, Jacob staggered to his feet and stumbled from the protective walls of the dog pen. His heart fluttered uncertainly, and his head ached from his recent labor and the heat. When he lumbered ahead to find the path he had just blazed regrown with goldenrod of even greater stature than before, he began to question his own sanity.

Lunging forward in desperation, Jacob attempted to uproot the nearest plants with brute strength. He yelped with pain and immediately withdrew his hands. A jagged cut neatly bisected his left palm along the lifeline.

The rustling of the saw-toothed leaves grew more violent still and blended with the buzzing of pollen-glutted insects. The sun glinted mockingly from the disk and ray florets. The earth began to spin beneath the man's feet. The gaudy plants towered over his head. Then there was nothing but cool silence.

Aaron Shotts dozed fitfully at his writing desk and then woke with a start. Was that a scream or just his sodden brain playing tricks on him? Aaron leaned back in his chair to stretch his knotted shoulder muscles. Because he hadn't slept much in over a month, his face was now a mere caricature of its former self. His eyes were sunken and lusterless. His mouth drooped idiotically.

A faint rustle passed through the open window, and the old man glanced warily at the lengthening shadows spreading across his den. After noting the blood red reflection of the late evening sun dancing on the wall, he mumbled aloud, "Maybe I'd better go over and see how Jacob made out with his path-clearing project."

Aaron stamped woodenly across the yard that separated his split-level home from Jacob's identical residence. When a shudder passed through the sea of yellow flower heads bobbing in the backyard, he spotted a few single goldenrod stalks sprouting from his otherwise well-trimmed side yard. Funny, he thought, those weren't there yesterday. Quickening his pace, he made a mental note to return and uproot the pesky plants before they could choke out the grass between the houses, as well.

The lanky, old man climbed onto his neighbor's

front porch and rang the doorbell. An ominous buzz echoed briefly through the house. After several minutes' wait, Aaron rang again. This time the hum did not cease when he removed his finger from the button. Finally, he creaked open the door and called out, "Jacob. Jacob? Are you--"

Aaron's voice strangled with terror when he found the living room transformed into a hive of buzzing insects. His eyes were drawn from the open window that admitted a steady stream of pollen-laden bees to the hexagonal patterns of honeycomb that encrusted the four walls and ceiling. It was then that he first noticed the low, almost human howl emitting from the backyard.

Aaron backed down the porch steps without closing the front door. Once his feet touched the ground, he bolted around the corner of the house and lunged neck-deep into the goldenrod jungle. As he thrashed toward the distant dog pen, the goldenrod stalks sprang to an even greater height in his wake. If his neighbor had cut a path earlier that afternoon, there was no evidence of it now.

The air was so heavy with pollen that Aaron's breathing came in rattling gasps by the time he had reached his objective. What he found just outside the steel mesh enclosure of the kennel was enough to stifle his breathing altogether. There, beneath a swarm of feasting bees, lie Jacob Martin, his big bald head tilted back against the fence. It didn't take any coroner to tell he was dead. His vacant eyes stared skyward in the most ghastly fashion, and there was a hint of yellow powder around the corners of his mouth. The powder was the exact color of the flower heads that towered over the corpse. Conversely, the flesh of the dead man's face was the dull, bluish shade of a strangulation victim.

A shiver passed through Aaron as the sun set behind the distant oak-ridden hills. There was another sudden howl followed by a sharper rustling of the goldenrod.

AN UNFINISHED PUZZLE

The sky is a Ouija board of bright stars.
Frost glows on the frozen lane,
and wolves glide ghostly from a thicket.
Owls worry the marshes with their calls.
The night is an unfinished puzzle
with plenty of pieces missing.

ANTIQUE TOYS

Walter glanced suspiciously about as he limped up the steep lane through a grove of withered thorn trees. Not even a peddler had stopped by in weeks, yet the old recluse still could not shake the feeling that someone was trespassing on his land. The last time he felt this uneasiness, he had caught the Johnson kids raiding his fish pond. Then, about a month ago, it had saved him a dozen of his best chickens from the hands of thieving Gypsies. They had sure dropped their gunny sacks quickly enough when, shotgun in hand, he had surprised them in the henhouse and dusted their drawers with buckshot. Now, he chastised himself for leaving the old double-barrel leaning in the corner behind the wood stove.

Walter quickened his pace, spurred on by a glimpse of red brick through the scabby trees. His house sat atop a small knoll that overlooked his twenty-acre farm, and the wizened hermit was out of breath by the time the pointed gables were plainly in view. The dwelling had been quite grand twenty years ago when his wife was still alive. She had seen to it that the shutters were freshly painted each spring and was forever scrubbing the flagstone walk and brick porch. Now, those same shutters sagged on corroded hinges, and weeds overran the walkway. With only his own footsteps to keep him company, there was no longer any reason for Walter to brighten the path with flowers or to sweep the crumbling flagstones.

The old man shivered when he stumbled across the threshold and into the shabby living room. It was almost as chilly inside the house as it had been patrolling the moors beyond the barn. Snatching up a poker, he went to the pot-bellied stove in the far corner and pried open the stove door. He detected a few glowing embers that he fed with wood shavings and finely split kindling. It wasn't long before the fire roared and sputtered, and the room began filling with that smoky heat so welcome on a damp spring day.

Walter mopped some clammy sweat from his face with a handkerchief before collapsing into a moth-eaten horsehair chair beside the stove. Still chilled, the hermit pulled his coat closer to him before leaning forward to warm his fingers. Afterward, he glanced worriedly about the room, taking note of the tattered carpet, stained wallpaper, and dusty shelf of antique toys hanging behind the stove.

It was then that his intuition began to nag him again, stirring up blurred Gypsy faces and firelight memories dead for twenty years. As the old man's gaze froze upon the ball and jacks and carved locomotive on the shelf, a single tear rolled down his weathered cheek.

He wondered why he had ever permitted those roving bandits to camp on his property that summer so long ago. After all, had his own father not confirmed the Gypsies' affinity for horse stealing and kidnapping? Maybe Walter had been swayed by their beguiling smiles. On the other hand, maybe he had just needed the rattle of their tambourines and their laughter to drive his dead wife's pneumonic cough and feverish blue eyes from his head. How could he have known they would leave him lonelier still?

Suddenly, there came a rattling at the front door. Before Walter could recover from his surprise, the handle turned and two swarthy men entered with hats in hand. The eldest had kinky dark hair and wore an earring in his left lobe. When he smiled, there was a flash of gold that outshone the mischief lurking in his dark eyes. He checked out the room in an instant, not missing Walter's stealthy glance toward his shotgun leaning in the corner.

It was the appearance of the younger visitor, however, that startled the old man even more. He was a lad in his early twenties with a dark, wind-burned face. Although, like his companion, he wore baggy clothes and a bright kerchief tied around his neck, that was where the similarity ended. Walter had never before seen a Gypsy with blue eyes and a pug nose!

After a moment, the middle-aged stranger cleared his throat, and a very sad expression passed over his face. "Kind sir," he began, "we two find ourselves stranded down by your front gate. Our wagon broke an axle, and we are without tools. Would you, kind sir, have any timber about that might serve as a temporary axle until we catch up with our brethren? We would gladly pay."

Walter glanced skeptically from one swarthy figure to the other and then rose slowly and--with that warning voice screaming inside him--began inching toward his shotgun.

"I don't think I can help you," mumbled the old man. "Why don't you try the next farm down the road?"

Before Walter could sidle around his chair, the younger Gypsy, on cue from his partner, strode to the stove, between Walter and his double-barrel, and stood warming his fingers.

"Even if you could lend us a saw, a hammer, and a few spikes, we would be most grateful," wheedled the lad.

"I'm sorry," replied Walter, turning to face him. "I think it'd be better if you'd just leave."

"Oh, you do, do you?" snarled the Gypsy blocking the front door. "I think it's time you learned how Marco and me deal with inhospitable wretches!"

Walter crouched low as the bigger man leaped at him from across the room. He hit Walter and drove him headlong into the pot-bellied stove. The stench of singed flesh and hair bit at the recluse's nostrils. A searing pain jackhammered its way through his scalp.

Crumbling to the floor in a swoon, he heard his attacker cackle, "This old man. We teach him to shoot Gypsies, eh, Marco? You fill our sacks. I take care of him! I make him sweat. Eh?"

The younger man produced a burlap sack from beneath his poncho and began to fill it with pewter mugs and silverware that he snatched from a rickety bureau. As he ransacked the room, he felt a definite sense of deja vu. It startled him to unearth treasure after treasure in such a purely routine manner. In other robberies, he would have had to demolish the dresser to find the money he had somehow known was taped to the bottom of the middle drawer.

His partner, meanwhile, had tied the unconscious old man to his horsehair chair before pushing it against the stove. The back of the chair had already begun to smolder while the Gypsy fed load after load of kindling wood into the fire.

This was the part of the job that the younger man found hard to stomach. So what if the old guy had shot up a couple of the brethren for swiping some chickens? He still could not understand this eye-for-an-eye vengeance that was so ingrained in the other members of his tribe.

As Marco shuffled past the slumped figure of the old man, he noticed for the first time a shelf of antique toys hanging above the shotgun in the corner. In a daze, he pulled down several wooden jacks and turned them over and over in the palm of his hand. While doing so, a strange prenatal stirring caused him to turn and more carefully examine the stubbly face of their captive. There was something vaguely familiar about that high brow, square chin, and pug nose that even a three-day growth of whiskers couldn't disguise. When the lad's gaze drifted back to the miniature locomotive on the shelf, a puzzled frown rippled across his forehead.

The other Gypsy removed a glowing poker from the stove and swaggered over to Walter. As the Gypsy struck the old man twice across the face with his closed fist, Marco snatched up the shotgun and leveled it at the hermit's chest.

"What are you doing with that gun?" growled Marco's partner. "You don't plan to shoot him, do you, boy? That surely would attract the neighbors."

"What do you plan to do with him, Sol?"

"What do you think?" Sol replied, waving the hot poker suggestively over Walter's bare wrist. "Have a little fun. Eh?"

Spurred by the cruelty of the other's smile, the boy cocked the shotgun and pulled both triggers at once. Buckshot ripped through the old man's vitals, turning them into hamburger. Walter jerked awake just long enough to recognize the deeper sleep that numbs forever battered faces and third degree burns. When he slouched forward, eyes vacant and staring, he did not feel the bonds cut into his wrists.

Sol reeled backward with the shotgun blast

ringing in his ears. There was a panicked look on his face when he whimpered, "What kind of Gypsy are you? Don't you know that murder will bring the law and outsiders among us? Now, we're going to have to make a run for it!"

Marco stared stupidly at the gun in his hand before allowing it to slip with a clatter to the floor. "At least we burn the old man, so his soul will not wander," he said by way of apology.

Without looking at the corpse, Marco wheeled around to snatch up the bag of stolen goods. He was about to make his exit when he heard Sol mutter, "Don't forget those antique toys. They'll bring a good price."

The lad rushed behind the pot-bellied stove and scooped the ball, jacks, and carved train engine into his gunny sack. As he did so, a curled, brown photograph fluttered from the shelf into his outstretched hand. When Marco drew it closer to his face, a light of recognition glinted in his blue eyes. The picture showed the old man he had just murdered sitting on his brick porch with an infant cradled in his arms. The baby, in turn, was clutching a tiny toy locomotive.

A primeval scream rattled from Marco's throat. The baby in the curled, brown photograph was HE!

LUKE THE SPOOK

"Do you really think there'll be any parkers at Willowdale tonight after all that's been happenin' out there this week?" asked Billy Miller, tugging on the football jersey that greatly constricted his bulging biceps.

"Do werewolves bay at the full moon?" chuckled Adam Andrews with a wink as he steered his jalopy around a sharp curve on West Washington Street. "It's Friday night, ain't it, man? What else is there for all the groovy couples ta do with no football game or school dance goin' on 'til tomorrow?"

"Even after WKBW sent a reporter all the way from Buffalo to check out that Luke the Spook story that's been all over Bradford High?" protested Miller from the backseat of the speeding vehicle "Do you really think that anybody'd have the hair to go make out in such a scary place now?"

"When the hormones call, the hormones call!" chortled Al Sykes, riding shotgun.

"Yeah," seconded Andrews. "Why should anybody be afraid of a dummy set up at a tomb by boys in white sheets? At least that's all that the cops said they found. We pulled better pranks than that last Halloween. Don't you remember how we scared the crap out of those little kids by droppin' firecrackers in their candy bags? Why, there was candy blown all over the road after their sacks exploded and they ran bawling to their mamas."

"That was a real blast all right!" laughed the blonde hulk, Gator. "Knockin' down Old Man Johnson's pumpkin head scarecrow wasn't bad either, even if he did chase us for six blocks."

"Yeah, but nobody's gonna catch us rugged football players!" brayed Adam. "We are Owls, the mighty, mighty Owls!"

"That's right!" seconded Gator, putting a playful headlock on Miller in the backseat. "We're gonna kick the Warren Dragons all over the field tomorrow! With me, Al, and Billy blockin', an' old Hammerhead Andrews runnin' the ball, we can't lose!"

"That is if we make it back before curfew," cautioned Billy after fending off Gator. "Remember. We gotta be home in bed by ten o'clock."

"Certainly," chuckled Adam. "After we catch our quarterback makin' a few passes at Betsy Jo, Tammy, or whoever else he's scorin' with, we'll head back pronto."

"Heck, Hammerhead, I'm surprised you didn't take Molly out parkin' tonight," snickered Gator.

"Watch your mouth!" barked Adam. "I wouldn't even think of takin' the girl I'm gonna marry out to Willowdale! I've dated Molly since ninth grade, an' she's the only one I ever wanna be with. Wait 'til ya see the dress she's gonna wear to the homecoming dance. She's so beautiful an' good an' loving an' kind an'--"

"Ah, knock it off," interrupted Billy, making gagging noises in his throat. "You pussy whipped guys are all alike."

"Yeah, knock it off," shouted Al, "'cause there's Willowdale just up ahead! It'll be a real trip howling through them steamy car windows. I even brought my Herman Munster mask. I'll let you wear if you want, Adam, since Molly let ya off your leash."

Andrew's jalopy squealed around a sharp curve and started up a straightaway toward two ponds that marked the entrance to a bleak graveyard. When the headlights danced on the black water, Sykes cackled, "Look. There's where they bury the sailors."

"Ha. Ha," said Billy with a sick grin. "I'll bet jokes like that got more than one commodian planted up here."

Just past the ponds, Adam slammed on the brakes before making an abrupt right turn into a narrow lane. Slowing to a crawl, he drove through a labrynth of dense shrubs and shadowy tombstones. Here, he clicked on his highbeams and proceeded with extreme caution. The cemetery road wound back and forth through the black evergreens and laurel for a good two hundred yards. The gloom even stifled Al's usual patter.

Finally, the jalopy crawled past a row of scaly, white birch and emerged into an open field cluttered with fresh graves.

"Looks like lots of people are just dyin' to get into Willowdale," chortled Al, noting the recent additions.

"Yeah, some old boys really dig bein' here," joked Billy with a nervous laugh.

"These stiffs got moved from Corydon," said Gator. "Otherwise, they'd have been buried under the Kinzua Dam."

"Damn water, anyhow," guffawed Sykes.

"Will you shut that pie hole of yours!" hissed Andrews. "How do you expect to sneak up on any parkers brayin' like them yokels on Hee Haw?"

"And how do you hope to get close to 'em with those highbeams shining from here to Allegany State Park?"

Flushing, Adam Andrews turned off all but his parking lights and dropped his car into first gear. Inching up the cemetery road, he guided his vehicle past a giant, pointed obelisk that had been erected in honor of the town's industrial magnets, the Dresser family. Still having encountered no other vehicles, he drove left toward a distant mausoleum glowing ghostily in the moonlight. The square vault sat secluded near the edge of the woods. Its eerie phosphorescence accented the horror of the place amid the suffocating shadows.

"Hey, there's the Luke tomb," said Billy in an awed whisper. He produced a pair of binoculars he used to spy on parkers and trained them on the far vault. Suddenly, he gasped. "L-L-Look! The door windows are busted, a-a-and there's vines growin' up the one side. Is there really any use goin' up there with all the rumors an' all?"

"Sure!" replied Adam. "A trail alongside the tomb is where most parkers hide. Don't tell me that the same right tackle who eats defensive ends for breakfast is spooked by a little gossip?"

"No. No!" assured Miller. "I-I-I just wanted to save you from. . .uh. . .wastin' gasoline. Remember we only put in 50 cents worth before we come up here."

With a derisive chuckle, Andrews drove directly for the mausoleum that sat with its back to a gloomy pine forest. Waxy-leafed laurel bushes grew on either side of the gray marble structure, and a hidden brook gurgled softly from a thicket to its left. When Adam saw that the trail beside the tomb was empty, he muttered, "Looks like we're out of luck tonight boys. Might just as well head back to the big B town and flame the Main. That is if you fellas can pitch in for more gas. I can't believe gas has gone up to a whole twenty-four cents a gallon!"

The words were no sooner out of Andrew's mouth, when a misty figure floated around the side of the mausoleum and headed straight down the pine-bordered trail toward them. The apparition was transparent, and yet it had substance like a sunbeam full of dust. One of its appendages motioned for the football players to get out of the car. The next thing Adam knew, he was slamming his jalopy into gear and was spinning gravel all the way out of Willowdale Cemetery.

The pals sat speechless until they were headed back down West Washington Street for Bradford. Finally, Gator said, "W-W-What was that thing?"

"L-L-Luke the S-S-Spook!" stuttered Billy.

"A-A-And he wasn't wearin' no sheet!" gasped Al.

"Ah, I think we let our imaginations get the best of us!" growled Adam Andrews.

"Then, why did you peal out like that?" asked Gator.

"It was just some kinda. . .reflex. Heck, it's still early. Let's go back and have us another look."

"Why, not?" chuckled Al, whitefaced but with his sense of humor intact. "Bein' that none of us crapped our knickers, I guess we're still good to go. Here's another 50 cents for gas. I'm in. How about the rest of you heroes?"

Grudgingly, the other highschoolers dug deep in their pockets and handed Adam more change. Clutching the money in his big paw, Andrews drove downtown to the Rocket gas station and pumped a few more gallons in the tank of his jalopy. With a determined scowl, the burly fullback paid the attendant, squeezed back behind the steering wheel, and bombed off toward Willowdale with his grim teammates hanging on for their lives.

This time Adam parked in the open field housing the fresh Corydon graves. He barely screeched to a stop before he and his buddies bailed out of the car. Each boy was armed with a flashlight and a varied degree of courage. While Adam struck out boldly for the mausoleum at the edge of the woods, the others seemed content to stay well away from any place shadows crept from the hedges.

Gritting his teeth, Andrews strode up the graveyard road, crunching gravel beneath his feet. He made no attempt at stealth as he stomped toward the tomb. His eyes swiveled nervously. A river of sweat rolled down the middle of his back. It's just like them pregame jitters he told himself. After first contact, I'm fine. Hand me the ball. Let me crash through the two hole. Smash into somebody. Confront. . .the ghost. I'll be fine. Fine!

The full moon bathed the tomb with bright light, and the name "Luke" stood out in bold chiseled letters from the glowing granite. Adam bit his trembling lip and kept walking as the nightmarish vision burned itself into his brain. It was then that the same apparition he had seen before from the safety of his car came floating out from behind the mausoleum. This time there could be no doubt what stood before him. Not more than twenty feet away, a gleaming, legless manshape in a blue tuxedo hovered above the ground. An airy carnation adorned the ghost's lapel, and his fuzzy features filled Andrews with heart-pounding fear.

When the phantom closed within five feet, Adam felt his legs melt from beneath him. As he writhed on the ground in absolute terror, the beckoning spook floated so close that the football star could almost reach out and touch it. Finally, Adam let out a shriek and began crawling for all he was worth toward the distant flashlight beams. Although he couldn't manipulate his legs, he still made good time. All he knew is that he dare not look back as he scrambled away on all fours, clawing madly at the cemetery lawn.

Al, Gator, and Billy recognized their fullback's shriek and charged off through the glowing graveyard to rescue their friend. The last time they had heard him yell like that was their sophomore year when Adam ended up at the bottom of a pile and got spiked in the face after being separated from his helmet. They held their flashlights like guns as they veered around tombstones and patches of laurel. Finally, they saw what they at first thought was a big dog scrambling madly toward them.

"It's Adam!" gasped Sykes as his flashlight fell on the approaching figure. "Adam, what's wrong?"

When Andrews recognized Al's voice, he recovered his legs, sprang from the ground, and sprinted off toward his car. Immediately, his teammates wheeled around and ran as hard as they could to keep up with him. It wasn't until they were crammed back in the jalopy with the doors locked that Adam managed to stutter, "L-L-Luke was after m-m-me.

A-A-After me!"

"Then let's leave!" urged the bug-eyed Miller, hugging himself with his huge biceps. "What are you waitin' for?"

Adam slumped over the steering wheel fighting for his breath. Finally, he said, "No, we gotta go back!"

"Go back?" echoed his teammates.

"Yeah, all season Coach Powers has been teachin' us to be men. Remember how he told us that the only way to fight fear is to face it headon? Without lessons like that, we'd never be 8-0 with just two games to play."

"Yeah, they don't call Powers 'The Rock' for nothin'," replied Billy with a fearful grimace.

"And if we don't leave now," added Gator, "the Rock's gonna fall on us for missin' curfew!"

"Hey, it's only 9:15," growled Adam after glancing at the luminous dial of his wristwatch. "We've still got plenty of time to return to the tomb again before Coach calls our homes to do his bed check. Besides, I know how you guys are. If I don't go back to Luke's, it'll be all over school how much of a chicken I am. How will I get any votes for homecoming king if everybody's laughin' behind my back?"

"Hey, we won't tell a soul," swore Al, barely hiding a smirk.

"See. I told ya. Are you boys comin', or not?"

"I guess so," grumbled Gator. "What choice do we have, with you doin' the drivin'. Let's just make it quick."

With Adam in the lead, the football players trudged once more in the direction of Luke's tomb. The moon played hide-and-seek with the clouds, often plunging the boys into a darkness that their flashlights barely penetrated. When they arrived at the mausoleum, they looked more like a herd of skittish deer than brave gridiron champions.

"Hey, I don't see nothin'," mumbled Billy Miller after they poked around for a couple seconds.

"Yeah, let's split," said Gator, shining his flashlight into a dense patch of pines directly behind the mausoleum. "Old Luke musta turned in for the night."

"I-I-I don't know," stuttered Al. "L-L-Look over there in them laurel bushes."

Al pointed off into the darkness toward a pair of red eyes that glittered from the gloom. The eyes shone with a hideous intensity that turned everyone but Andrews into walking Jello.

"Hey, I ain't runnin' this time," grunted Adam, "Let's git 'im!"

Swinging his flashlight like a sword, the fullback strode boldly into the brush directly toward the glowing orbs. His teammates only followed to keep from getting separated from their spiritual leader. As soon as they began to move, the eyes did likewise. When the guys speeded up, the eyes speeded up; when the guys slowed down, the eyes slowed down. Somehow they could never quite close on what was luring them into the dense forest.

"It looks like we ain't gonna catch old Luke," whispered Billy after they'd gone several hundred yards.

"Yeah, this is useless," agreed Gator. "If we get lost in the woods, we'll miss our curfew for sure."

"Okay," growled Andrews. "Let's go. At least now nobody can say I'm a damned sissy."

The other football players exhaled relieved sighs and began backtracking toward Luke's tomb. The going was difficult through the thick brush that tripped them at every turn. The ground was very broken, which caused them to fall frequently. That all changed when Billy happened to glance back into the deep woods and saw that the red eyes were now hunting them. He gurgled a warning before bolting like a panicked beast. Soon his teammates were running, too, dodging the dim-outlined trees as if by radar. They leaped ditches they never would have dared hurdle in the daylight, following their flashlight beams back to the tomb that now shone like a welcome beacon in the moonlight.

The panting football players burst from the woods and collapsed like a derailed train on the trail next to Luke's mausoleum. They lay in a tangled heap with their chests heaving and their breath rattling in their throats. They were up again in an instant, but before they could sprint to the safety of Andrew's car, a shadowy figure stepped from the darkness behind them and barked, "I thought you boys were supposed to be in bed by ten o'clock. Don't you know it's already five after?"

"C-C-Coach Powers?" gasped the players in unison. "W-W-What are you doin' here?"

The Rock held up two flashlights fitted with red bulbs. "I heard some of my players were involved in this Luke the Spook thing that everyone's talking about. I had to find out for myself if that were true."

"Then, it was you who's been scarin' the heck out of us?" groaned Adam sorrowfully.

"Yep, and it looks like you boys will be sitting out tomorrow's game with the Dragons. And the Erie Strong Vincent game, too."

"B-B-But how can our team go undefeated with four of its starters on the bench?" protested Al Sykes.

"Yeah, if we don't win them last two games, there'll be lots of disappointed Owls' fans," mumbled Gator sheepishly. "There hasn't been a Bradford team that's gone undefeated since. . .1961!"

"You should have thought of that before you put yourselves before the team," snarled the coach. "I hope you learned a valuable lesson here tonight. To be a winner, it's necessary to focus on team goals instead of foolish fantasy. I'm really disappointed in you. Young men of your intellect should know that there's no such thing as ghosts!"

"Then you better tell h-h-him that!" stammered Billy Miller, pointing aghast off through the moonlight. A gleaming, legless manshape in a blue tuxedo had just floated beckoning from behind Luke's tomb. An airy carnation adorned the phantom's lapel, and its fuzzy features had the same substance as a sunbeam full of dust.

MACABRE DREAMS

Macabre dreams
rack my nights.
The bizarre feast of
out-of-body first love
blends with spooky
forests & fire spewing
from closet maw.
Her lips are so real
I can taste their kiss.
I plummet backward
thru yearbook black hole,
snapped from sanity's chain.

GRADUATION DAY

As Adam dragged his pot gut up the cliff beside the waterfall, he began to realize how middle age had crept up on him. His legs quivered and his flabby biceps strained as he searched for handholds among the loose rubble. Ahead of him puffed two equally rotund figures who made just slightly better progress up the granite outcrop. Complicating matters for them all was the steady drizzle that seeped from the black clouds boiling above the mountain.

If it weren't for the scrub brush that sprang between the cracks in the rocks, Adam knew he could not have climbed a yard up an incline that twenty years ago would have not even challenged his athletic prowess. Actually, it was thoughts of his upcoming high school reunion that had prompted him to attempt this adventure. Al Sykes and Billy Miller had promised to guide him to the last wild trout stream in northern Pennsylvania where native brookies were still as plentiful as they had been in the late 60's. When they had showed up drunk that morning at his door, dressed in their letter sweaters and carrying antique telescopic metal rods instead of the latest ultralight equipment,

Adam figured his buddies were pulling one over on him in retaliation for dumping cement in their birdbaths. Now that he knew the price one had to pay to get to the best part of the stream, he wasn't so sure. What he did know was there wouldn't be any idiots on three-wheelers to ruin the fishing back here. And what the hell! Maybe he would even lose a few pounds and look more like the old ace fullback instead of old man Andrews, pus-gutted salesman for Happy Rest Mortuary Supplies.

After another forty minutes, Adam pulled himself to the top of the cliff and collapsed beside his two contemporaries. He was footsore, fly-bit, and fagged out. As he hit the ground, the flashlight in the back of his fishing vest clunked him in the kidneys. "Damn," he groaned, pulling the metal object from his pocket. "Why did you guys insist I bring this hunk of crap along?"

"You do wanna leave here tonight, don't ya?" winked Al Sykes as he swatted at a hovering swarm of black flies.

"Huh?"

"Come on, wimpbag!" exclaimed Billy Miller.

Adam's two friends stumbled to their feet and headed upstream. From the back they looked like rubber-skinned hippos, draped as they were in dripping rain gear. Momentarily, they disappeared in a fog bank that obscured the stream from view, and Adam followed the squeak of their waders for more than a half-mile before he thought he caught a glimpse of them disappearing into the entrance of an old mine shaft out of which the creek blackly bubbled.

"Hey, guys!" shouted Adam after them. "This can't be for real! How are we gonna catch any fish in a crummy old mine?"

Adam stood hesitating at the entrance wondering if it would be worse to wait there alone in the fog or follow his friends to God knows where. Only the eerie echoes of "Wimpbag!" made him plunge ahead once more.

Adam fumbled with his flashlight and then followed the dim beams of light dancing ahead of him down a slick trail that veered sharply to the left. The gurgling brook was quite close now as the passageway narrowed. Soon, the trail merged with the streambed, and Adam found himself splashing along a narrow tunnel eroded through dripping bedrock. He was about to turn around and head back to the car, wimpbag or not, when he saw a glimmer of daylight ahead.

Adam emerged squinting into a broad bowl-like valley. Here the creek, unpolluted by silt, meandered lazily between moss-covered banks through a forest of white oak. Surprisingly, no black flies pestered him, and the June sky was a brighter blue than he had ever seen it. Somehow, the storm that had dogged the fishermen up the mountain had dissipated during the half-hour they had spent in the mine.

Beside the stream Adam's two buddies were

unfolding their telescopic fishing rods and tying on hooks and sinkers. Adam was about to assemble his own equipment when he heard someone giggle off through the brush. Adam spun around half expecting to be the butt of some cruel hoax. Instead, he saw some picnickers coming down the trail from the woods. By the way they frolicked in the sunlight, he could tell they were teenagers even before he spied their long hair and love beads. Damn, dressed as they were in plaid and paisley, they could have just stepped out of Adam's senior yearbook!

When the kids got within a few yards of Adam, a blonde, muscular youth suddenly pointed a finger at him and shouted his name. The fisherman shook his head in disbelief. Standing there, looking just like he remembered him, was his best buddy from high school, who Adam hadn't seen since the kid split twenty years ago.

"Gator?" Adam gasped. "Why, it is you! You still look like one of the Beach Boys for cripe's sake!"

"Hey, Adam, what's happenin'?"

"Damn! Where have you been hidin'? Jack freakin' Lalaine's? Let me look at you. How have you stayed in such good shape after all these years?"

"I'm just a groovy kinda guy!" Gator snickered, flexing his biceps. He twisted slightly to keep Adam from seeing the wicked-looking scar that traversed his spine just below his muscle shirt.

"Gator, what in the hell are you doin' out here in

the middle of the boonies?"

"This place is outta sight! Like far out!"

"You got that right, buddy."

"Hey, man, there's a groovy little chick here that you're gonna get into seein'."

Gator motioned to a lithe blonde who had paused up the trail. She was the only teen who wasn't dressed like a hippie. She wore the same homecoming dress and white stockings that accented her figure in a way that had haunted Adam since high school. She came slowly toward him, as if from a dream, with her hands clasped over her pouty lips.

Adam cried, "Molly!" Then he found himself hugging his first true love, the one he had never gotten over, the only one who had ever really mattered. The news of her death in a dormitory fire over eighteen years ago now seemed very unreal indeed!

Adam felt the tears well up in his eyes, and he held his girlfriend so hard that he left welts on her pale arms. He still didn't understand why he had broken up with her on graduation day and let her go off to college without him. "I can't believe it's you," he sighed after a moment. "I can't believe. . ."

"Oh, Adam," sobbed Molly. "Please promise you'll never leave me again. Please!"

"Yeah," chuckled Gator. "Why don't ya stay here with us, man?"

"Hey, wait a minute there, bucco!" snarled Miller. "We came here to catch us some brookies."

"Adam, you don't wanna hang with Gator," cautioned Sykes. "He ain't been one of us since he burned his draft card and shoved off for the West Coast. Remember?"

Andrews noted his middle-aged friends' paunchy bodies huddled hippo-like beneath their steaming rain gear. Half moon wrinkles encumbered their eyes, and their furrowed faces spoke of ugly divorces, pressure sales, unpaid mortgages, and eight-hour waits in foreign airports. Repulsed, Adam turned back to his sweet love and brushed his fingertips across her cheek. Then, without another word, he took Molly's hand and let her lead him up the cool forest path.

Two flashlight beams probed the twilight as the middle-aged fishermen who held them splashed downstream. An empty creel slapped against each man's side. A steady downpour kept them shivering deep in their rain gear.

"What a rotten day!" growled Miller from beneath his soggy cap.

"Yeah! All this physical exertion crap and not one trout to show for it!" grumbled Sykes. "We oughta castrate the SOB who told us about this place!"

"Man, I haven't done this damn much walkin' since high school."

"It's too bad that Adam missed out on all the fun! What became of that weenie, anyway?"

"Hell, I don't know," muttered Billy. "One

minute he was followin' us through the fog, and the next minute he was gone. The wimpbag musta headed back to the car."

"Who woulda thought I'd see the day old Hammerhead Andrews would wimp out on anything?" said Al. "Man, how that kamikaze SOB used to crash into the line! Need a touchdown late in the game, just give it to old Hammerhead!"

"Yeah, he broke more helmets in preseason practice than the whole rest of the team did in ten games!"

"And how about the way Andrews kept going back to Luke's Tomb that night?" reminisced Sykes with a chuckle. "If old Luke the Spook hadn't showed up right after Coach Powers caught us breakin' curfew, we'da never led the team to an undefeated season. There sure ain't been any of those since high school, huh, Billy?"

"What I remember most," sighed Miller, "is how Adam bribed Rock Powers into keepin' us on the team. I can still hear Andrews say, 'If you don't let us play out the season, sir, I'm gonna tell everybody in school how you ran like a scared girl up at Willowdale.' Hell, it took us almost an hour to catch up to Coach before we could say anything to him. For a guy who didn't believe in ghosts, he sure skedaddled out them cemetery gates!"

"'Face your problems head-on,' always was Hammerhead's mantra," murmured Al. "Man, it really spooks me the way Adam's disappeared."

Finally, the men reached the cliff they had

scaled in the morning. Their descent required two free hands, so they put away their flashlights and inched their way down the bare granite, gripping the scrub brush whenever possible. It was fully dark by the time they reached the bottom.

Discerning the roar of the waterfall through the gloom, Al said, "Let's try the big pool below the cliff."

"Naw, what's the use?" grumbled Miller. "It's probably fished out just like the rest of this freakin' creek!"

"Ah, come on, Billy! Might as well as long as we're here. Who knows? Maybe there's a lunker lurkin' around down there."

"Are you into pain, or what, Al? I'm ready to collapse now!"

"Oh, I know. You just wanna get back to the car and keep old wimpbag Andrews company."

"Bite it, bucco! I'll come, even though I know it's a waste of good drinkin' time!"

The two men felt their way along the base of the cliff until they distinguished the glimmer of rushing water ahead. Miller fished a flashlight from his pocket and held it while Sykes rigged his pole. He was careful not to shine the light into the pool.

Al hooked a whole nightcrawler through the collar and cast it far out into the gloom. As the current caught it, he raised his rod tip to allow the bait to float naturally the full length of the pool. He was about to reel in and try again when he felt something heavy tug on the end of his line. Sykes set the hook, and his rod bent double.

"Holy crap! I snagged me a monster! Must be a holdover brown!"

"Don't horse it! Don't horse it!"

Miller held the light while Al splashed downstream to work his heavy catch ashore. He was so excited that he never questioned why it acted more like a northern pike than a trout. There were no slashing runs, no jumps, just a steady pull of dead weight as if it were conserving its energy for one final rod-jolting rush to freedom.

After many minutes, Sykes worked his catch onto the beach. Even a carp would have been welcome compared to what he found on the end of his line. It was Adam Andrews, lying faceup in the water. His eyes were open and glinted surreally in the flashlight glow. Somehow, his face looked younger--almost the same as it had on graduation day.

OTHER BOOKS BY WILLIAM P. ROBERTSON

Poetry Books:
Burial Grounds (Triton Press, 1977)
Gardez Au Froid (Triton Press, 1979)
Animal Comforts (Vega Press, 1981)
Life After Sex Life (Four Winds Press, 1983)
Waters Boil Bloody (Robyl Press, 1990)
1066 (Robyl Press, 1992)
Hearse Verse (Robyl Press, 1994)
The Illustrated Book of Ancient, Medieval & Fantasy Battle Verse (Robyl Press, 1996)
Desolate Landscapes (Robyl Press, 1997)
Bone Marrow Drive (Chuck's Electronic Press, 1997)

Audio Books (Co-written with ShadowFox):
Gasp! The Haunted Recitations of William P. Robertson (Robyl Press, 1999)
Until Death Do Impart (Robyl Press, 2002)

Novels (Co-written with David Rimer):
Hayfoot, Strawfoot: The Bucktail Recruits (White Mane Publishing, 2002)
The Bucktails' Shenandoah March (White Mane Publishing, 2002)
The Bucktails' Antietam Trials (White Mane Publishing, 2004)
The Battling Bucktails at Fredericksburg (White Mane Publishing, 2004)
The Bucktails at the Devil's Den (Forthcoming from White Mane Publishing)
The Bucktails' Last Call (Forthcoming from White Mane Publishing)

ORDERING INFORMATION

Several of William P. Robertson's poetry books are available online at ProjectPulp.com, while his audio books can be ordered from CDBaby.com. His novels can be obtained online from Barnes& Noble.com and Amazon.com or at many local outlets throughout northwest Pennsylvania. Autographed copies of <u>Lurking in Pennsylvania</u> and all of his other books are available from the author. For more information e-mail Bill at buccobill@webtv.net or write him at P.O. Box 293, Duke Center, PA 16729.

HORSES

Horses posed
in the mist
like lava statues
waiting to unthaw.
Smoke poured
from their nostrils
& their eyes glinted
with subtle fire.
Down the path
they jolted,
fading to
photo
negatives.